A Town Where Lights Are Blue

A Town Where Lights Are Blue

William Saffell

Quiet Storm Publishing • Martinsburg, WV

All Rights Reserved. Copyright © 2003 William Saffelll

No part of this book may be reproduced or transmitted in any form or by any means, graphic, electronic, or mechanical, including photocopying, recording, taping or by any information storage or retrieval system, without the permission in writing from the publisher.

This book is a work if fiction. Any resemblance to actual events or persons, living or dead, is entirely coincidental.

Published by Quiet Storm Publishing

For information, please contact:
Quiet Storm Publishing
PO BOX 1666
Martinsburg, WV 25402

Cover design by Clint Gaige

ISBN: 0-9714296-8-5
LCCN: 2002094972

Printed in the United States of America

Dedication

Thanks to my wife, Krisnajanti, for all her help and support, and for being my best friend. Thanks to my daughter, Jessie, for teaching me about one of the main issues of this story without ever talking about it. Thanks to my publishers, Clint and Darla Gaige, for believing in my worth as an author and for making the publication of this novel a reality. Thanks to two gifted writers, Robert Norris and Mary Triola, for giving me invaluable feedback, help, and kind words during the writing of my book, and for taking the time to offer two outstanding quotes. Thanks also to Gray Harris for reading this *towazugatari* ("unrequested tale") in a very raw form and seeing something of merit in it.

A Town Where Lights Are Blue

"There's a black river flowing,
There's a town where lights are blue,
There's a saying: 'love is darkness',
And I think it's mostly true..."

From "Inferno Of First Love"
By William Saffell

Chapter One

It was after midnight and raining in Yokohama. The music was over, and had been for some time when John Sky finally stood away from the piano. The bandstand was empty of people, save him, and most of the Akabashi's employees had gone home, or at any rate had left, long ago. He stood looking at the pictures that covered the walls around the bandstand. It had started out as only a couple of photos and posters, until Sky and his partners in the band, as well as assorted bar employees and patrons, began making contributions. He glanced over pictures of Charlie Parker, T-Bone Walker, Louis Prima, Stan Getz, Gene Vincent, Otis Redding, Dave Brubeck, Groove Holmes, Ben Webster, Shirley Scott, Jim Pepper, Gene Krupa, and many others. He looked at each picture slowly and carefully, though he had seen them all many times.

His sidemen were sitting at a nearby table, playing cards and drinking brandy. It was their way of relaxing after the end of the last set, when the energy that had built up over the course of an evening's four sets was slow in diminishing. Tsushima, the owner of the Akabashi, sat with them, going over the night's receipts, his fingers moving rapidly and skillfully along the beads of his old abacus, looking for mistakes, though they seldom surfaced. He was drinking coffee and looked absorbed in his work, but Sky knew from long observation that this amounted to his way of unwinding after a night's business.

"Have a good night, boss?" Kenji, the drummer, asked, and Tsushima looked over at him and frowned at having his concentration disturbed. The Akabashi's owner was a short, disheveled, and bearded man who not only owned the Akabashi but also appeared to live in it, but Sky knew this wasn't the case. He'd been to Tsushima's house plenty of times. Some men had women, some had liquor, some had gambling, and some had music. Tsushima had the Akabashi, and Sky doubted that many people or things were loved more. He seemed out of place in the city at times, coming as he did from the small island off the coast of Kyushu that had also become his namesake. Tsushima frowned and lit a cigarette, ignoring the talk going on around him as Yasujiro, the bassist, laid down a full house-jacks over threes-and picked up the handful of bank notes that made up the pot. "I knew my luck had to change sometime," he said, smiling as he took a sip of his brandy.

"I don't think mine's going to, at least not tonight. Let's get going. It's still early enough to have a little fun," said Mikio, the guitarist and youngest member of the group. Sky smiled as he sat on the edge of the bandstand, a glass of beer close at hand. He had heard this conversation, or variations of it, countless times, but the fact that it was predictable didn't annoy him. On the contrary, he welcomed its constancy.

"Want to come along?" Yasujiro asked, and Sky shook his head.

"Thanks all the same, but you fellows try to get along without me tonight," he said, standing up quickly and unsteadily. He loosened his tie and rolled his shirtsleeves down, the thing that he always did when he was getting ready to leave after work. His partners knew that he always wore long-sleeved shirts, but invariably rolled his sleeves up as soon as he took his jacket off, just before he sat down at the piano. As Kenji had once noted, you could almost set your clock by it. When Sky rolled his shirtsleeves down it meant that he figured to leave soon, no matter where he was or what he was doing.

"Got any plans?" Tsushima asked.

"Just get a bite to eat, a couple of drinks, then head on home. That's about it," Sky replied, and Tsushima nodded, although he doubted what he'd heard, because Sky was drinking, which probably meant that he wouldn't get home until after dawn. That was his way, and everyone at the Akabashi knew it.

"You sounded especially good tonight. I really liked the last set. What was the name of that new tune?" Tsushima asked, and Sky smiled tiredly.

"New for us, maybe. It's an old standard, boss. Been around for years. Everyone's played "Angel Eyes" at least once, though some have done better by it than others. It's expected of a piano player if you play in a joint like this. Thanks for the kindness, but did you catch Mikio's solo toward the end of that number? As solid and cookin' as anything I ever heard," he said, and Mikio, who, in spite of his dark tailored suit and air of world-weary self-assurance, looked more boyish than ever. He smiled, pleased but embarrassed by the praise.

"It was pretty cool," Kenji said. Like the others, he wore a carefully tailored suit and a silk tie. His sidemen made Sky, whose black suit looked like a relic of the early sixties, look shabby and outdated by comparison. They had, however, long ago given up on trying to convince him to pay more attention to his wardrobe. In fact, they no longer cared. They did what they did, and he did what he did. A wide gulf often existed between Sky and his partners in the quartet, but it never surfaced in their music. That always came out as four voices, one sound. Just what the patrons of the Akabashi wanted and expected to hear.

Sky cleaned his glasses on his wrinkled striped tie, causing Kenji to wince, and he thought for a moment about going along with the others. He then decided to stick to his original plan. He figured their asking him along was another example of their kindness toward him. He also figured that they probably planned to meet some girls somewhere later on, and he couldn't imagine fitting into such a scene without some awkwardness. He paused by the back door and began buttoning his overcoat. He felt almost dizzy for a moment, overwhelmed by fatigue and the smell of cigarette smoke, sweat, mingled brands of perfume, and both recognizable and exotic kitchen odors drifting in from the back. He hooked the handle of his umbrella over one arm and his cane over the other as he lit a cigarette.

"See you boys later," he said, and the four men at the table waved. He then pushed the door open and walked out to encounter a thin but steady rain falling into the alley. He walked down the alley and past the few bars that lined it, some open and some not, as bits of paper and gritty dust blew by him, carried by the strong wind.

Sky had known that it was raining long before he entered the alley, although nobody he had spoken with during the course of the evening had said anything about it. The metal that the army doctors hadn't been able to get out of his left leg, as well as some metal of their own that they'd inserted, had let him know that it was raining from the middle of the second set. He seldom thought much about his damaged leg, except on nights like this, when the weather made it unavoidable.

Sky passed no one as he walked through the alley, but he occasionally heard music or laughter coming through the doors of the still-open bars. He could hear sirens wailing in another part of Yokohama, but their sound was faint. He paused when he came out to the street and wiped sweat from his forehead. His leg throbbed with a dull and rhythmic pain. He looked first one way, then the other, before moving on. It was cold, though only the middle of November, but blue lights shone through the rain from an all-night spot a few blocks away, giving him enough reason to want to go there.

A Town Where Lights Are Blue

Chapter Two

In the dream, Sky's mother had been alive. Laughing and vital, filled with all the many and at times contradictory emotions that he knew her to possess. Not dead from exposure and alcohol poisoning in a ditch two hundred yards from the front door of their house on the Crow Reservation in Montana. She died a few weeks after her thirty-fifth birthday and a few days shy of his fourteenth.

His mother's name was Maria Sky, but her Indian name was something much longer. It was something like Sky Shakes Wind At Morning, or so she had told him. She had shortened it to Sky for ease of use. She had traces of French and Italian ancestry mixed in with her Indian blood, from long-departed visitors to Montana, perhaps having come there from long wanderings beyond Canada. Her skin, as Sky remembered it, was a kind of gold-olive-brown, and her hair was deeply, intensely, black. Growing up, it seemed to him that she looked much the same as all of her neighbors, friends, and relatives on the reservation. In later years, however, he could see this wasn't quite true. In some light she looked Mediterranean, while at other times she looked almost completely East Asian. He still recalled an incident during a furlough in Saigon, when he had been drinking with a Korean corporal in a Tu Do Street dive. The Korean soldier brought out his wallet and showed him pictures of his family, and the picture of his wife had given him a chill. The young woman bore a striking and disturbing resemblance to his mother, although at the time he chalked it up to being drunk.

His father had been a few years older than his mother, but the age difference was never the cause of any problems for his parents. His father was of Dutch-Jewish ancestry, the son of immigrants who had settled in the far northern region of North Dakota, very close to the Canadian border. As the story that Sky had heard growing up went, he had worked off and on for bootleggers bringing illegal liquor across the border before the repeal of prohibition. He had, however, also worked many other jobs. At one time or another, his father, Jacob, had worked as a ranch hand, truck driver, gas station mechanic, and telephone lineman. He had also been, for a time, a middleweight boxer with a fair record and more than a few knockouts across two dozen pro bouts. Many people felt that Jacob was an unlikely choice of mate for Maria Sky, but Sky knew that his parents shared many things, both obvious and subtle. They loved their part of the West, if for different reasons. They shared their need for alcohol. They were also deeply in love with each other. Sky came across some of their correspondence from the war years, and their deep closeness was made clear in the simple yet profound way in which they expressed their feelings.

His parents had fought loudly and often. According to his Uncle James, who took Sky in after his mother died, his father often threw harsh words, often inanimate objects-but never punches-at least at his wife. His uncle made it clear to him that his father had more than his share of flaws, and he had a violent side, but he also pointed out that this didn't extend to hitting women or children. James told him once, as they paused on the prairie digging post-holes, about a fight his father had been in. Sky's parents were drinking in a bar somewhere off the reservation when a huge, drunken man insulted Maria Sky. The man was an oil field roughneck, headed south, and Jacob had fought the man all the way across the bar, out the door, and into the parking lot, where he finally put him down with a series of short, sharp jabs. His uncle didn't always speak of Sky's father in positive terms, but he told this story with a mixture of respect and admiration.

His father had his last furlough in the fall of 1943, a few months before Sky was born. Jacob had heard stories, some true and some not, about the German Army's mistreatment of the Dutch people, Jews in particular. He was eager to be trained as a rifleman and get to Europe, hopefully Holland, where he'd be able to kill as many enemy soldiers as possible. He was over thirty and not in the best of health. In truth he could have probably avoided active service. Sky knew, however, that he didn't just want active duty, he demanded it. His father became a rifleman, and apparently a courageous soldier, but he never got close to Europe. The army sent him to New Guinea. He fought there in a bitter campaign against the Japanese in perhaps the harshest terrain of the Pacific War. He was wounded twice and he also contracted malaria. As rough as his trials on New Guinea were, however, they didn't stop him. He survived them all only to be killed coming in under heavy defending fire in the invasion of Luzon in 1945.

Sky's mother got a visit from two somber uniformed soldiers after her husband's death. Her mother asked them in and gave them coffee. She noticed some livid red scars trailing away into the collar of the younger man's shirt, but the young sergeant was calm and sincere as he expressed his condolences. The two soldiers gave her stiff but kind words, a folded flag, some folders filled with personnel files, and his father's ribbons, medals, and badges. His mother never displayed any of these decorations, but Sky still remembered her, in the years after the war, taking them out and looking at them. She would sit in the kitchen, drinking straight whisky and listening to mystery programs on the radio. She looked over each ribbon, medal, badge, and patch, taking them carefully from the old cigar box in which she kept them. As she did this, her face underwent slight and subtle changes. Her expression indicated tenderness, anger, loss, longing, and combinations of feelings known and felt only by her. His mother was never obvious about it, but she let Sky know that he should keep the memory of his father with him at all times, even if they hadn't been able to spend any time together. He had never known his father, but he felt like he had. When he was growing up, and even later, after his mother died and he moved in with his uncle's family, there was always a picture of his father in the house, not necessarily prominent, but nevertheless there. Years later, when he was on patrols or under enemy fire in Vietnam, he felt like he shared a special kinship with the father he'd never had the chance to meet. Sky's mother had once told him that Jacob had paid a price few people would ever have to even think about paying. He wasn't a saint, but he'd done good things all the same. In some ways he envied his buddies who had mothers, fathers, wives, and kids back in the states, but on the other hand he wouldn't have traded his situation with anyone in his outfit. His parents were long gone, yet they had left him a legacy nobody could take from him. They had given him their love and their tough knowledge of a beautiful but imperfect world, and it served him well, through his boyhood, during his time in the army, and even into his stay in Yokohama.

The dream had faded almost completely as Sky stood by the window, remembering and forgetting. The house was cool and quiet. It wasn't raining, but the air was damp, and his leg ached. The walk across the room had taken some effort, but the pale sunshine made him feel glad. He looked for things he knew. The narrow street beyond his tiny yard was still there, as was the canal just beyond it. He hadn't gotten much sleep, and he badly wanted a cup of coffee to strengthen the as yet slight sensation of consciousness that coursed through him. Having slept later than he usually did, he realized that he'd have to start getting ready for work soon. He felt hungry, sore, and alone, but also grateful to be standing there, leaning on his cane by the window, reconnected to the solid real thing that Yokohama had become to him.

A Town Where Lights Are Blue

Chapter Three

Judging by the talk, laughter, and music coming down the stairs toward him, Sky figured that the B&W, the bar where Ota worked, was as crowded and lively as usual.

Ota had been Sky's friend since his first visit to Yokohama. He came down to the city on his first furlough from the Camp Zama hospital, after months of treatment, therapy, and recovery. He had spent quite some time practicing walking with a cane, but the city made him forget a lot of what he'd learned. It was with some difficulty that he negotiated the steep, narrow stairs of the B&W, standing to one side as people came up or down. They looked at him, at times with sadness or pity, at other times with indifference. He walked by the large sign on the right side of the stairwell that read, in both Japanese and English: NO AMERICANS ALLOWED. He saw the sign but never paid any attention to it. The B&W looked like an interesting place, and he'd been determined to go there. Once inside, he never saw signs of any ill-feelings directed toward him.

The B&W was nondescript, much the same as hundreds of other bars in Yokohama. It consisted of a long, narrow room with a bar, a few tables on the far right side, and a jukebox to the left that played both American and Japanese pop songs. Sky couldn't think of anything that made the place special. He went there because it was where Ota worked.

Whatever the reason or reasons, the two became close friends immediately.

Ota was young-looking, but he was actually a few years older than Sky. He had introduced Sky to a wide and varied circuit of bars and nightspots. He also introduced him to several people, all of whom, as a rule, were friendly toward him. The kind of nightlife that Ota showed Sky was new to him, but he took to it at once. He got away from the hospital as often as he could and caught the train down from Tokyo many times.

Ota and Sky shared an instantaneous affinity, but on the surface they didn't appear to have much in common. Ota was from a big city, was totally urbane, and felt at ease in just about any setting, whereas Sky knew only farm life on an Indian reservation, playing music in small towns, and the army. Whatever it was that brought them together, it was real, and they maintained it, even after Sky's transfer back to the states.

Ota saw him as he came in and waved him toward an empty seat. Sky sat down and ordered cognac with an ice water back and brought out his cigarettes. Akemi, one of the part-time bartenders, came over to light it for him. She greeted him and then moved on as a new group of customers came in.

"Busy night at your place?" Ota said. He wore, as always, a white shirt, black pants, and a dark tie. His hair was as short and neat as Sky's was long and unruly.

"About like usual."

"Try out any new tunes lately?"

"Not since "Angel Eyes," but "You Don't Know What Love Is" is coming along well."

"I'll stop by some time and check it out."

"It's going to be a while yet."
"You staying until closing?"
"Not tonight. You got any plans?" Sky asked, and Ota smiled in a way that made him think that he had met a new and interesting woman.
"We're going out to a party. Akemi's birthday. Want to come along?"
"Sounds like fun, but I think I'll go on home after this."
"I'll come by the house in a couple of days."
"Do that. I found some Hank Mobley records you might like."
"I'll do it. I'll bring Hisako along."
"Hisako? Haven't heard about her," Sky said, smiling. Ota had lots of girlfriends, and he was always meeting new ones.
"We just got together recently. We get along all right. You seeing anybody?"
"You never leave anybody for the rest of us," he replied, and Ota laughed, then moved on to take care of other customers.
Sky finished his drink and paid up, then remembered to give birthday greetings to Akemi. He paused on the street in front of the B&W. The street was still crowded and noisy in spite of the hour. None of that seemed to have anything to do with him, however, and he realized he should probably just head for home.

A Town Where Lights Are Blue

Chapter Four

Sky played piano at the Akabashi five nights a week, Tuesday through Saturday. The bar was open on Sunday and Monday, but the band had these nights off. The quartet often rehearsed on Sunday and Monday afternoons, and he spent many unpaid hours there arranging sets or going over new songs by himself. Sky and his partners played many kinds of music, but mainly a mix of jazz, rock and roll, and rhythm and blues. Local jazz fans or American servicemen occasionally sat in on saxophone or trumpet, and once in a while someone asked to sing, but most of the music was instrumental.

Sky had started to play music when he was still in high school. He had to work after school on his uncle's farm, but he began to make time to work on teaching himself how to play piano. As far as he knew, there was only one instrument in the area-an ancient, battered upright in the high school auditorium. Miss Keeler, who had taught music at the school for many years, tutored Sky from time to time. Her favorite songs were classical pieces and show tunes, and she taught Sky many of these, after he had spent long hours and days on the fundamentals. He also got some help from his aunt, Sarah. She seldom talked about her love of music, but her skill and passion for it was made clear the first time she reluctantly went to the auditorium to coach him. Aunt Sarah loved jazz, blues, and boogie-woogie, and she was skilled in all of them. And, so, with the combination of genres imparted to him by his two teachers, he developed a good ear and a sure sense of time. He realized that he had no other talents or skills. He only had music.

He joined a band right after high school, and they traveled to a number of states, as far south as Arizona, playing a mixture of honky-tonk, jump blues, and the newly emerging genre called soul. They played mainly bars and roadhouses, and he learned a lot from his sidemen, most of whom were much older than him. Most of them were self-taught. They gave the impression of being a cynical and undisciplined group, but Sky knew that they were very focused when it came to practicing and playing music. They drank a lot, but it never affected their ability to play. Most of the hard drinking came after the last set, and Sky was usually in on this. He worked steadily and sent money to his aunt and uncle every couple of weeks. He called home every ten days or so. He was in a phone booth in Reno when he called his uncle and got the news about the arrival of his draft notice. He quit the band the next night and went back to Montana.

Sky usually showed up for work at seven, but the first set didn't begin until nine. There'd usually be only a few customers around when he came in, and he spent time going over set lists, looking over sheet music for new songs, and having a few words with Tsushima. The last set ended at two, and he'd usually stay around for awhile and then head for the all night bars, often staying out until after sunrise. It was on such a night that he first encountered Sayoko.

He had first seen the young woman in the Akabashi a few weeks earlier with another girl about her age, which he guessed to be about twenty-one. They were in the company of two men in their forties. His immediate impression of the girls was that they looked like they worked in one of the big cabarets in Yokohama.

There was something about the taller of the two girls that attracted Sky from the first time he saw her. Her features were typically and classically Japanese, yet there was something intangibly different about her. Her flawless complexion was slightly dark, and her shoulder-length hair was shot through with a darkness that was beyond blue-black. Her eyes were wide and bright, and he sensed some secret in them, something intriguing and special. It was this perceived secret that most appealed to Sky.

The quartet had finished the third set, and an American airman had sat in on tenor saxophone for the last couple of songs. His sidemen went to a table to talk jazz with him, while Sky took his beer and sat at a table close to the stage. He felt tired, as he often did after a set, but also good. They had played very well that night. He was leaning forward at the table lighting a cigarette when the taller of the two cabaret girls paused near him. She didn't speak, but she nodded in his direction and looked ready to say something when she abruptly walked away with lithe movements and a sudden laugh. She left the Akabashi in the company of the other girl and the two men shortly after the beginning of the last set.

Sky left the bar after sharing a drink with his sidemen, who stayed behind to talk to Tsushima and the saxophone player. The conversation sounded interesting, and the young serviceman appeared to know a lot about jazz, but Sky was restless and wanted to move on.

The night was his element, but he felt detached from it

as he walked down the alley away from the Akabashi. Light snow flew around him, carried by a stiff wind, and he burrowed deeper into his faded black overcoat, unable to stop thinking about the story in the tall girl's odd, sad eyes. He came out to the street and caught a taxi to a bar across town.

町 光 青

    The bar was crowded and noisy when he arrived. He ordered a beer and sat down to take in the scene. Most of the people in the place looked young and they all seemed to be having a great time. He hadn't been there long when the two cabaret girls came in. They were no longer in the company of the two men. They both looked to be in high spirits, and more than a little drunk. He found out from the bartender that the tall girl's name was Sayoko, although the man was reluctant to give any further information. He took in the news and tried to think about music as he settled down to his drinking.
    Sky didn't stay in the bar long after Sayoko and the other girl arrived. On his way out, he saw Sayoko point in his direction and laugh, as her friend and their two new male companions joined in. In his long coat, feeling exhausted, and with his cane striking the floor in an unsteady rhythm, he felt hopelessly ungainly.

Chapter Five

The room was very cold, and everything in it had a warped and unfamiliar appearance. Sky's vision was blurred in a transition between sleep and consciousness. Sitting up slowly and putting on his glasses, he realized that he had fallen asleep beside the *kotatsu* in the living room and not in the warm, comfortable futon in the bedroom. The *kotatsu* was a modern one, with electric heat instead of the traditional charcoal brazier, but it had been turned off long ago. He remembered coming in and sitting down, then lying down with the intention of sleeping only a few minutes. His overcoat had been pulled over him, and he pushed it aside as he sat all the way up, his head throbbing and his eyes aching.

The room now took on the familiar dimensions that he had come to know well. He didn't have much furniture in the room aside from the *kotatsu*. The main thing was an old stereo system and dozens of record albums along the walls. He bought records just about every time he went shopping, although he'd tried to cut down on this in recent months. An old blue armchair sat next to a floor lamp across from the *kotatsu*. He usually sat there when listening to records or the radio while reading.

The house was chilled through with the penetrating cold characteristic of some Japanese cities near the sea. He attempted to stand up, but the metal pins in his leg felt welded into place, and he sat back for a moment, sweating in spite of the cold, and waited for another try.

When Sky got the wound that ruined his leg, he had already been wounded twice while on operations with his unit in the Ninth Infantry Division. His outfit would often spend long stretches in the field and have many men killed or wounded, but few were actually shot. In fact they often went days without seeing the Viet Cong and still suffered heavy casualties. Most of his friends who had who been killed or wounded were victims of booby traps: trip wires, punji pits, or "Bouncing Betties"- mines that popped up to waist level after being tripped and then detonated. The Viet Cong had many other types of booby traps at their disposal, but these were the ones he recalled most vividly.

Sky's first two wounds weren't especially serious, but they were certainly painful and frightening enough. He took small arms fire in the shoulder in an ambush near Fire Support Base Moore and later caught some shrapnel in a mortar attack at Binh Phuoc. He was actually in the division base camp at Dong Tam when he received his third and final wound. In the GIs' parlance it was a million dollar wound-the kind that got a soldier sent home. He was glad to get out of the fighting at the time. Later, however, lying in the Camp Zama hospital, thinking about the past that had brought him there and the future that seemed increasingly uncertain, it began to seem less and less like a good thing.

His outfit had been given a couple of weeks at the base camp when he drew guard duty. All enlisted men shared this responsibility. It usually consisted of perimeter guard in the bunkers along the berm, but security procedures also required that guards be placed at the petroleum dump and the airstrip, where soldiers and the brown water sailors of Task Force 117 came to catch flights to Saigon on propeller planes called Caribous. It was a simple piece of hard-packed earth covered with perforated steel plating and a shed-like terminal off to its rear. Sky arrived there at two AM. The guard at the air force weather compound greeted him as he took up his post and told him to head for their place if they got hit, because they had a bunker. Sky thanked him and began his shift. He checked the inside of the building and then walked outside to take a look at the landing strip. The moon was big and bright, and there were no clouds in the sky, but everything that he saw looked indistinct and not quite real. He was making a pass around the building when the first rockets slammed inside the wire, scoring hits on the orderly room and barracks of one of the helicopter companies on the northern end of the perimeter. Sky recognized the sound as that made by 122 millimeter rockets, and they quickly started coming south across the base in the way the GIs called "walking." He was on the far side of the landing strip shed when the rockets started coming in and he moved quickly toward the relative safety (safety to him meant being out of Vietnam altogether) of the air force compound, but he never made it. He was hit when he came around the side of the building and lay there until two airmen came over and pulled him into their bunker. He recalled seeing helicopters flying in and out of the camp, buildings burning, and hearing the sound of eight-inch guns returning fire. After that came long months in a hospital in Japan. He then flew home and got his discharge. He recalled his confusion and surprise when a group of young people at the airport smiled at him and some other returning soldiers, and it came across as a welcoming gesture. Later, as Sky and the other soldiers passed by them, they asked the newly arrived veterans how it felt to be murderers and how many women and babies they had killed. He thought that maybe they were drunk or crazy, or both. He had seen women and children in Vietnam, but his outfit was kept busy with trained regular troops. While some of them may have been young, just like many of the GIs, they were all adults as far as he knew. He didn't know then about the anti-war movement. His knowledge of that came later, as did the realization that nobody was more anti-war than soldiers in combat zones. He had thought about his home in Montana, his aunt, his uncle, and his cousins, the same as brothers and sisters to him, in every spare moment during his time overseas. He found it hard to express his feelings about his experiences in Vietnam, but he'd never thought of himself as pro-war. He'd been given a responsibility, and he accepted it. He had also paid a price, but he thought of that as his own business, and more often than not he kept it to himself.

Sky shook his head and stood up. He reached down and got his watch off of the kotatsu and saw that he needed to start getting ready for work. A scalding hot bath in the Japanese manner and a few cups of black coffee made him feel better. By the time he had knotted his tie he knew he was ready to go. He put on his coat and walked out across his front yard, up the side street and out onto the crowded boulevard beyond. He entered a noodle stand and ordered his usual meal of fried rice and tea.

町 光 青

The Akabashi was crowded that night. People streamed in all through the evening and everyone appeared to be in a festive mood. Sky went through the motions during each set and even his aloof sidemen gave the impression of being more enthusiastic than him. He couldn't strike a groove. He felt at odds with the piano, and therefore lost.

The night went by quickly, and he was pleased to see it come to an end. His music usually consumed him, but on this night he hadn't felt like a part of it. He was met outside after closing time by Ota, who had with him a stunning young woman of mixed French and Vietnamese blood named Simone Tre. She had been living in Singapore for some years and was in Japan for business reasons. They stood outside the club for awhile, talking and shivering. Yasujiro came out and the four of them went out for drinks. Ota and Yasujiro laughed when Sky ordered coffee. He left them after a short time in the bar and returned home through the windy night.

A Town Where Lights Are Blue

Chapter Six

It was a particularly cold Thursday night, and Sky thought that the quartet could do no wrong. Everything had gone right, more than right, from the first notes of the opening set. The people who came into the bar that night responded heartily to the fire and energy of the band, and a few patrons came up during the course of the evening to try their hand at singing. Not all of them were especially good, but they made up in feeling for what they lacked in skill and everyone seemed to enjoy it.

Sayoko came in shortly after ten o'clock in the company of a young man dressed in a stylish dark suit. Sayoko wore a long, pearl-colored dress, and she looked lovely and full of life and high spirits. She danced with her companion, her hair flying, as she moved in sinuous patterns against the surging beat. She looked happy. The quartet broke into a waltz and everyone danced.

町 光 青

Sky stuck around for his customary one drink, but his partners were too keyed-up to settle into their usual post-gig card game. They ordered whisky, then stood around the bandstand, laughing and talking. They talked about certain solos and songs that had gone especially well. "You Don't What Love Is," a song that they had struggled with in rehearsal, had finally come together for them, and they hadn't even meant to play it. Sky had simply gone into an introductory solo, and the bass and drums had seamlessly followed him after the first few bars. Mikio's entrance into the song was flawless, just a few single-note lines, and then they were into it with no looking back. Sky's solo had stretched out longer than was customary for him, and it was as if he didn't want to let it go, hanging on to a repeated phrase, but only just long enough. No one danced during this song, but everyone in the bar applauded and cheered when the last notes died out, quietly and perfectly.

Sky left the Akabashi in the company of his sidemen, and they were all exhausted but elated, in too good a mood to let it come to an end. People had bought them drinks all during the night, and they were all more than a little drunk in a warm, happy way. They walked down the alley singing "Shina No Yoru" in off-key harmony, laughing as their breath made swirling vapor patterns in the dim light. They walked until they found an all-night cafe that suited them. The place was crowded and throbbing with the rhythms of night people in their element.

町 光 青

Sky had no idea where he was when he woke up later that day. He lay fully dressed, except for his coat, in a *futon* that took up most of the space in a room scarcely bigger than a closet. He looked around for his glasses and then laughed when he realized that he had fallen asleep wearing them. He recalled barhopping with his partners and staying out until well after sunrise. He felt a sense of regret at having to leave the small but comfortable room, but he knew he had to get up. He opened the sliding door and walked into the living room of what turned out to be Mikio's house. A young woman, wearing what looked to be the shirt that Mikio had been wearing the night before and nothing else, sat gazing at a television set, riveted to the screen by the plot of what looked to Sky like a mid-1950s science-fiction film about a giant spider on a rampage in the Southwestern desert. She absently pulled alternately at her long hair and a strand of pearls she wore. She sipped a cup of coffee and paid no attention to a cigarette that was burning itself out on the table in front of her. She was completely oblivious of Sky and everything else except the movie.

Mikio and the others drifted sleepily into the room one by one, all looking disheveled and tired, but also happy and serene. Two young women filed out later on, talking among themselves. In time, everyone, even the girl who had been entranced by the monster movie, wandered out to the dining room and converged around the table. Sky noted that Mikio's house was small but neat. Sunlight slanted in through the two windows in the room, giving it a warm, pleasant glow. Two of the girls went into the kitchen, and soon the smells of boiling coffee and frying eggs wafted into the room. The girls eased back in their chairs, and Sky went over to look at some woodblock prints on the bare tan walls. They looked traditional, and Sky felt that he had learned something about Mikio, that maybe everything didn't have to be up-to-date and with-it to have value to him. The third girl joined the others in the kitchen. Sky's partners in the band lounged and joked, often referring to Sky good-naturedly as "Old Man," as the early afternoon moments passed languidly by.

A Town Where Lights Are Blue

Chapter Seven

The bullet train that Sky rode sped through the countryside as rapid-fire bits and pieces of Japan filtered in to him through the misted windows. He was traveling from Yokohama to Osaka, but he had a sensation of passing through not so much a distance of space, but of time. People boarded the train from stations that gave the impression of growing naturally out of the cold dark earth. Most of the passengers who boarded the train at such places were country people with sober expressions. They wore aged overcoats or jackets over rough rural clothes, although some of the women wore simple yet striking *kimono* whose dominant colors ran primarily to earth tones. They often carried bulky bundles tied in bright cloth, and they invariably lit their cigarettes with wooden matches from boxes that had been painted and patterned and lettered in English script and Japanese calligraphy. These boxes of matches made him think of his tiny house in Yokohama. Its interior was littered with dozens of them, full or partially full, lying hidden or in plain sight like shards of memory. The matchboxes were an integral part of the Japan he had come to know. As for the train he rode, it was just one of the many trains he had traveled on while living in Japan. They all merged into one always-moving train that now made its way through cities and across barren fields, as Sky hurtled through a patchwork of earth

A Town Where Lights Are Blue

and time to buy a Yamaha piano in Osaka.

町 光 青

Back in Yokohama, in the same December vastness, Sky was insulated by a kind of temporality that he felt was peculiar to musicians, who always had their own unique outlook on time. It wasn't like any known to other people. It was past three o'clock and everyone had left the Akabashi except him. Sky wove his way tentatively through pieces of pop tunes whose lyrics-words that he could never sing-signified for him the strangeness that often infringed on everyday life. His chords lost their quality of uncertainty and became stronger and more assured as he ran the rim of dissonance to achieve an effect suitable for his mood. The room was lit only by the dim red glow of the exit lamp. He experienced a total but pleasant sense of melancholy in the dark and empty bar. He began to incorporate fragments of Beethoven's "Moonlight Sonata" into songs about contemporary sadness. The songs invariably contained lyrics making references to you. This made sense to him in commercial terms, but it otherwise came across as an alien concept. He wondered what *you* meant, and knew that for him there was not and had never been such an entity. There was no *you*.

Chapter Eight

The South Island Bar pulsated with life and activity. Flashing lights created ever-changing patterns on the faces and bodies of the soldiers and bargirls who moved through the crowded space. The jukebox glowed with pale pastels as it poured out defiant waves of American pop/rock/soul music. The bar catered primarily to soldiers on leave from Vietnam and Korea, so Sky's presence there made him feel like an outsider, yet he occasionally felt drawn to the place.

The patrons of the South Island kept the jukebox going nonstop with a never-ending flow of fifty and hundred yen coins. The volume was turned up high, so conversations had to be shouted. The bar was just a vast, dark room with red walls that were covered in some spots with movie posters and paintings that seemed to Sky to be in remarkably bad taste. Couples danced on the dark hardwood floor near the jukebox in an aura of perfume, sweat, and smoke. The bargirls preened in the wraparound mirrors on the walls and flitted through the mottled semi-darkness in bright miniskirts, boots, and floppy hats. Sky sat among the people at the packed bar, talking to soldiers and their girlfriends. He drank beer and smoked and dispensed coins to feed the jukebox, though he made no selections himself. In time he met a young black soldier named Earl. He was with a helicopter unit in Vietnam, but he didn't seem interested in talking about that. Earl wore a leather coat over a red knit shirt and black pants and was in the company of a quiet bargirl named Carmen, who wore a black dress and sunglasses with thick black lenses. She was pleasant enough, but she wasn't interested in the conversation being carried on between Sky and her boyfriend.

"So, how long you lived here?" Earl asked, and Sky had to lean in close to hear him.

"Not too long."

"Don't you ever want to go back to the world? You know, go back home?" Earl said. It was a perfectly understandable question, yet the word 'home' was without meaning to Sky. His home was a few miles away, down a quiet street alongside a canal.

"Once in a while."

"I know you're not a GI. But you were, right?"

"Years ago."

"Don't see many white dudes in here," Earl said, and Sky felt a rush of confusion and surprise. Is that what he was? White? He supposed that was the impression he made on people. He was white, but also other things. The mixing of his parents' blood had resulted in his being without any defining ethnic characteristics. His skin didn't look as dark as his mother's had been, but he'd never thought of it as white. He had gray eyes and brown, unruly hair, much like his father's had been.

"I guess not. I just come in now and then to listen to the music. I play piano in a place across town."

"Oh, yeah? What's the name of the joint?"

"The Akabashi. Come in sometime. My group doesn't play tonight, but we'll be in starting tomorrow," Sky said, but he doubted that he would see Earl after he left the South

Island. Although the Akabashi saw its share of servicemen, R&R soldiers seldom went there.

"Could be, could be. What kind of jams y'all lay down?"

"It's supposed to be mostly jazz, but we play lots of different stuff."

"I'm a soul man, myself, but I get a taste for something different now and then. Say, where you from back in the world?"

"Montana," Sky said, and Earl called for another round and laughed.

"People live there sure enough? I'm from Motown. You know, Detroit, and I'll be makin' that scene in fifty-seven and a wake-up."

"That's pretty short."

"There it is. The way I look at it, I got skate time coming when I get back. Two purple hearts is enough for anybody, and I got mine. Check me out in the rear with the beer. Yeah. Well. Maybe. Sounds good, anyway, don't it?"

Sky nodded in assent. "Sounds great," he said, hoping that Earl could get his wish. Sky understood the feeling. He knew by looking into Earl's eyes that he'd seen plenty of combat. With luck, he could spend some time in the rear as he finished his tour, but they both knew it wasn't a sure thing. They also knew that being in the rear didn't necessarily mean that people weren't going to try to kill you.

Sky finished his beer and said his good-byes. He came out to the street to encounter a light snowfall and bitter cold. He took a few deep breaths, trying to cleanse his system of the South Island's stale air. It was still fairly early in the afternoon, but the sky had turned dark with what looked like the promise of a storm.

A Town Where Lights Are Blue

町 光 青

    Sky continued drinking after he left the South Island until the darkness of evening finally fell. He drank only beer, though vast quantities of it. He drank in bars, noodle stands, cafes, and outside sake shops all over Yokohama. During the course of the day he talked to old men, off-duty bargirls, pimps from Yokosuka, lost European tourists, Korean sailors, policemen, and American soldiers and marines. He drank so much that he got to that disturbing level of drunkenness when a strange and unsettling feeling of sobriety begins to emerge.

町 光 青

    At eleven PM on his long day of drinking, Sky walked down the side street leading to his house feeling drunk, cold, and alone. He entered his house after fumbling with his keys for what seemed far too long. Thoughts and images of the day drifted through his mind. Some of these came across as stark and vivid and some lost their reality even as he thought about them. It was like looking at pictures whose colors were running in the rain, or maybe in the intense heat of a bright afternoon sun. In the midst of all this he tried to conjure up images of Montana, but none took shape. Had he ever been there? Had he ever really left?

    He sat down heavily in his faded blue armchair and rubbed wind-ripped hair away from his face. He then stood up abruptly, his cane sliding down and away onto the tatami at his feet. He looked down and smiled, nearly laughed, when he realized that he hadn't taken his shoes off yet. He'd been drunk plenty of times, but never to the point to where he'd overlooked that. Pain brought lines into his face and he stopped smiling. He then lurched forward and kicked a large glass bowl that had stood on the kotatsu for a long time. It was just something he'd picked up as a souvenir of a long-ago trip to Kyoto, yet it wasn't without meaning for him. The bowl exploded into countless blue and white shards, and these crunched sharply as he walked through them, with only the pale light of the late autumn moon illuminating the room. He then staggered back and slumped into the chair, staring out the window, out onto the road by the canal, into the dark and the cold wind.

A Town Where Lights Are Blue

Chapter Nine

It was a wild night in the Akabashi. People sat and stood two deep at the bar and all of the tables were full. People crowded onto the dance floor and still more people came in. The quartet had slammed through two sets with tremendous energy, and they now played a current American rock song that had an insistent R&B beat. A traveling English tourist handled the vocals, and Mikio and Sky took extended solos. The rhythm section sounded tighter than usual, and Sky noticed with some amusement that his sidemen had broken out in smiles, an unusual occurrence. He also noticed a rare and intoxicating air of excitement that spread through the place, spilling out across the flashing lights, motion, smoke, and general noise.

The alley that led away from the Akabashi was windy and cold. Sky had sudden thoughts of the main room of his house, empty of people. He envisioned the *kotatsu* cluttered with a collection of late weekend debris: a half-pack of cigarettes next to a box of wooden matches from a bar near the harbor, quart bottles of Asahi, scattered ten yen coins. A scent of dying chrysanthemums hung in the air, and light from the one small window let in cold, alien light. He broke free of this vision and came back into the song. It ended in loud, ironic moments frozen in bittersweet joy, lost among tired smiles, sweat, the flow of liquor, laughter and applause.

Screams of electronic feedback began to subside, and dancers began to move toward liquid and rest, exhausted but suffused with elusive happiness.

町 光 青

Sayoko sat on her living room floor alongside her *koto* instructor, Mrs. Noguchi. Her teacher wore an understated yet beautiful *kimono*. To Sayoko, she was like a cherished fragment of a forgotten past with no purpose other than imparting a sense of lost and sadly unwanted beauty. Mrs. Noguchi wore her hair in an elaborate style that Sayoko felt was well-suited to the wearing of *kimono*. She couldn't remember when she hadn't taken lessons with this graceful middle-aged lady. It seemed like a long time, and she hoped that it would go on for at least as long a time.

"Sayoko, it's refreshing to find in times like these a young woman like yourself with such reverence for old ways. I think it's wonderful that you've kept up with your lessons. I know how busy you are. Your technique is improving. You have a nice touch. You make mistakes, but we can correct those. The feeling is there. Don't lose it. Tell me, do you still take your lessons in flower arranging?"

"Yes. I still take them, but I'm afraid that I'm hopeless. Almost as bad as my struggles with playing music."

"You're being modest. I know better. You'll persevere. I know it," Mrs. Noguchi said with a kind of quiet certainty and finality that Sayoko found impressive and moving.

"I'll keep trying," she said.

The *koto* lesson continued, and the smooth-flowing music created by the two women became an achingly beautiful interlude in the bleak cold of the gray afternoon.

町 光 青

Other music came out of Sky's window, poignant responses from eight cellos and a lone, pure soprano voice: "Bachianas Brasilerias #5." He was tired and unshaven, wandering without purpose through the dark silence. His house had become a shambles of empty beer and whisky bottles, crumpled packs of a dozen brands of cigarettes, remnants of meals, and discarded or forgotten articles of clothing.

There hung in the air of the house an odor of moments and dreams gone bad, an atmosphere redolent of some sort of sober and joyless aftermath. The party was more than over. It had been erased from memory. He had tried without success to reach an outlook of rueful humor or ironic introspection, but he neither saw nor felt anything comical or philosophical. The house, in being emptied of its long-gone revelers, had become a messy, disheartening place, and the mismatched people who had departed for ostensibly happier scenes hadn't been brought there for any purpose that he could bring to mind.

Sky walked through the litter of his house with a headache beginning to come into full flower and his eyes squinting without interest or insight through the bad light and splotches on his glasses. He stopped suddenly, his eyes on a treasured organ-saxophone jazz LP that had been smashed to pieces. He thought that it might be time for changes, but he didn't know what shape they might take. Many people had passed through his house in the past few days, yet he could recall only a few faces, hardly any names. Even Ota had left. Christmas was coming, and he thought that might mean having some moments to enjoy, although this seemed like only a kind of conditioned response of long standing. He moved toward the chair and turned on the lamp, then turned it off again as he sat down. He preferred the soft pale moonlight as a companion. He sat down and tried to empty his mind of all thoughts as eight cellos and a voice of crystalline beauty flowed into the winter void.

Chapter Ten

On a snowy day before Christmas, Ota walked with Sky on a back street not far from Sky's house.

"You can tell that Christmas is coming soon. Can't you feel the excitement? Pretty soon everyone will be getting those big holiday bonuses. I think some good times are on the way," Ota said as they walked along.

"I guess you're right. There's something in the air, all right," Sky replied in a distracted tone.

"That's for sure. Say, do you remember last Christmas, when we wound up down in Atami?"

"How could I forget? It was quite a time. One of the best times I ever had, even if I was stone-broke for about two weeks after that. It was worth it, though. You know, Ota, I don't think I ever saw Miyumi look so happy, or so beautiful. You two looked so right for each other. I thought you were going to get married," Sky said, and Ota smiled, then looked away as though he couldn't think of anything to say. The fading afternoon was bleak with a damp and penetrating cold.

町 光 青

The bars and nightspots of Yokohama were filled to all

hours in the days before Christmas. The Akabashi had a big crowd every night, and the B&W had been very busy and raucous the couple of times that Sky stopped in after work. Sky and Yasujiro had been to a few bars, and they had all been crowded and lively. They entered one near the Akabashi and found it to be no less energetic than any of the others they had been in that night. They had been drinking beer, and they were in a good mood when they came inside.

"You know, Sky, I'm going to ask one of these lucky girls to dance with me," Yasujiro said just after they sat down and ordered their first round.

"Suit yourself. I'll just sit here and take in the atmosphere," Sky said as he reached for his beer. Yasujiro got up and began circulating around the bar.

The bar had bright pastel walls and a deafening jukebox. People crowded the bar and all of the tables, and the bartenders worked quickly and methodically to keep up with the steady stream of orders. A number of couples danced to blaring music at the rear of the room. Most of the people looked young and intoxicated not only by the steady-flowing liquor, but by an elusive current of joy that pervaded the place.

Sky smiled when he saw Yasujiro dancing with an attractive young woman dressed in trendy Western clothes. He brought her over to their table after they had danced to a few tunes. He introduced her to Sky as Akane. He thought that she was pleasant and a little naive. She laughed in a guileless way and drank nothing stronger than iced tea. They got up to dance some more after a brief rest and some conversation with Sky.

"Good evening, piano player," Sayoko said to him as she stopped by his table, and he looked up, surprised.

"Good evening, pretty girl. Care to join me?"

"Well, I'm not sure why, but I think I will sit with you for awhile," she said, and sat down across from him in a swift and fluid movement. She ordered a gin and tonic with her eyes not on him but on the crowd.

"I don't believe I've ever seen you in here before, piano player."

"I've never been in here before tonight. My friend suggested it. Is this place one of your haunts?"

"If I say yes, will you come here often?" Sayoko asked, her voice low.

"Probably not. I was just thinking that the place doesn't suit you. To tell you the truth, I wouldn't be in here myself if my friend hadn't suggested it and I wasn't so drunk."

"You don't look drunk," she said, looking openly at him.

"But I am," Sky replied in a steady voice. He then looked up as Yasujiro and Akane returned to the table. Yasujiro introduced himself and Akane to Sayoko. The two women got along well instantly and they excused themselves, saying they'd return shortly.

"You've done all right for yourself," Yasujiro said, leaning back and taking a drink of his beer. He was smiling, but Sky suspected that he was only half joking. He looked over at him and leaned forward, shrugging his shoulders.

"I'm not so sure," he said, his eyes far away. He then looked up as the girls returned. They talked and drank for a time until Yasujiro and Akane heard the introduction to a song they liked. They got up and walked back to the dance floor.

As Yasujiro and Akane danced, Sky and Sayoko carried on a conversation that went in cryptic circles. Questions were posed, but most of the answers were vague and noncommittal. By four o'clock they were both drunk. She looked over at him in a way that struck him as both natural and impulsive and said, "Do you want to go to a hotel?" He said nothing at first. He sat in silence that was amplified by the noise and motion going on around them. He couldn't stop looking at her black/gold eyes, thinking that some kind of special sorrow seemed to shimmer just behind them.

"There's no need for that. I've got a house. We can go there. But, whatever we do, let's get out of here," he replied, and they got up and began putting on their coats. They paused for a few moments to say their good-byes and then left the bar.

町 光 青

Sky and Sayoko walked through the cold, windy streets until nearly dawn, when they arrived at a frozen, deserted stretch of coastline near the harbor. They walked in silence along the wintry shore as icy surf crashed and foghorns sounded. Some birds were flying out toward the open sea, and a ship sailed by, far out past a breakwater. The first lights of dawn began to color some ragged clouds along the horizon. They walked through a landscape of torn, useless fishing nets and patches of dirty snow. They talked very little, but Sayoko laughed from time to time at things she didn't wish to share with him. The walk through the cold air had forced sobriety upon them, and they saw the morning as if through clear and new-found vision. In time they began to feel an affinity for the sound of the icy waves, the smell of the cold, bracing salt air, and the incremental coloring of the winter dawn. They paused close to the water's edge and she put her hand in his and stood close to him. The wind tore at them and the intense cold found its way into them, but they experienced a sense of peace and well-being that was matter-of-fact yet miraculous.

町 光 青

They arrived at Sky's house by taxi later that morning, feeling tired but content. The house was cold and they collapsed onto the futon, coats and all, and fell asleep almost immediately.

町 光 青

The afternoon sun was pale among scattered clouds when Sky woke up. He could see Sayoko moving through the house with a sense of graceful assurance, cleaning and straightening as she went along. She stopped suddenly and smiled at him. He felt bad, but seeing her smile had a soothing effect that made him feel that he could get the edge on his hangover.

"You have a very nice house. Small, but pleasant. But, very messy," she said in a tone of gentle and only half-serious reprimand. She knelt down beside him, brushing at her hair as she smiled down at him. She then made a face that indicated displeasure. "I hope you shave soon."

"I will," he said, rubbing his hand over the stubble on his chin.

"Have you been up long? You don't look tired."

"I haven't been up long. I never feel tired. You know,

A Town Where Lights Are Blue

Sky, I thought you were ugly the first time I saw you, but maybe you're not so bad. I think I've known you for a long time. You got strange-looking eyes, Sky. Will you tell me something about them sometime?"

"What's that?" he replied, amused by her question.

"What's behind them," she said, her expression intense, her voice serious.

"If that's what you want," he said, taken aback by the seriousness of her manner. Sayoko looked at him, almost smiling, then turned and walked toward the kitchen.

町 光 青

In the evening after supper they relaxed around the *kotatsu*. She wanted to hear some of his jazz records, anything with piano. He noticed that she listened very intently to the music. It wasn't just background noise for her. It was clear to him that it had meaning for her. Later they just talked or listened to the wind. She still wore the black sweater and short blue skirt she had worn to work the previous night, and she sat with her bare legs tucked underneath her. Her mood was alternately lighthearted and serious. The wind kept up outside, and rain intermittently streaked the window.

"The sound of the sea carries much further in winter," she said. Sky nodded and leaned forward at the kotatsu, savoring the semi-darkness, the smell of the strong coffee she had brewed for them, and the gentle sound of the rain.

"Yes. I've noticed that. It's like something in the other seasons keeps the sound away."

"It's best in winter, but in all seasons I like to be near the sea."

"So do I," he said, looking at her. She was looking out into the night, through the rain, as though searching for the sea.
"Sayoko, it's very nice to have you here like this. Do you want to stay with me?"
She turned to look at him, her expression still distant.
"Yes. I don't want to stay here now," she said. She folded her hands on the *kotatsu*, and the closeness between them that he had sensed receded like a sudden tide.
"I understand."
Sayoko smiled. "I'm glad to hear you say that. The time isn't right. Maybe later, things will be better."

町 光 青

Sayoko left his house early the next morning. It was Monday, and a light snow had just started to fall.
"I'll see you soon. I'm always around," she said as she stood by the door, her voice soft, her eyes looking into his.
"All right."
"Maybe Saturday. One more time."
"Sure, Sayoko. That sounds fine."
"Take it easy, Sky," she said, and he watched her as she crossed the yard and disappeared down the street, mingling with people coming and going, on their way to work.

A Town Where Lights Are Blue

Chapter Eleven

The snow stopped on Monday, but then it began to rain. It was a cold and penetrating rain that got into the very woodwork of Sky's house. Ota stopped by in the afternoon for a brief visit. He was in the company of Miyumi, a slender, vivacious young woman he had known for some time. His relationship with Miyumi was somewhat unusual for him. Most of Ota's relationships with women didn't last very long. His brother Hiroshi also came along. Hiroshi knew someone who knew someone in the film industry, and he had worked as an extra in a number of movies. He had appeared primarily in science fiction or period films, usually as part of a crowd. He had never had any speaking parts, and he could rarely be glimpsed on screen, but he thought of himself as very much a movie star. He was a few years younger than Ota, yet he looked like the older of the two. He had dropped out of college during a period of political fervor, but he had recently become a student again. Miyumi went straight into the kitchen to make some coffee while Sky and the others seated themselves at the *kotatsu*.

"So, how's the movie business?" Sky said, looking at Hiroshi.

"A little slow right now, but I'm expecting work in an important picture going into production the first of next year," he replied, as though he'd have a major role in such a project. Ota smiled at Sky, who nodded. He'd long ago learned to let Hiroshi maintain his film star image. He knew that it had no basis in fact, but it was important to him.

"What's the name of the picture?"

"That hasn't been decided yet," Hiroshi said solemnly.

"Well, keep me posted. I'll make a point of seeing it when it comes out," Sky said, and Hiroshi, who regarded Sky as a fan, smiled.

"I will."

Miyumi came back into the room with coffee. She placed it on the kotatsu and then sat down beside Ota.

"It's nice to see you around the old place again," Sky said, and Miyumi, who was pretty in a quiet and unassuming way, smiled.

"I've missed being here. I've been kept busy at work, and my elder sister got married recently. I haven't had much free time. I'm taking some time off that's been building up," she said. Miyumi worked as an accountant for a large industrial firm. She often put in long hours at work. She also worked mainly straight day hours, making it difficult to arrange her schedule with Ota's.

"We're going to Kyoto right after Christmas," Ota said.

Sky looked up from his coffee and nodded. "Sounds like a nice trip."

"They asked me to come along, but I'm going to Tokyo for a few days. I've been invited to a big holiday party with a lot of the top stars," Hiroshi said, and Sky regarded this seriously.

"You don't want to miss that."

"It's important for my career."

"What about you, Sky? Want to come with us?" Miyumi asked.

"It's nice of you to offer, but the club has some big nights coming up. Tsushima expects us there just about every night this time of year."

"You going in tonight?" Ota asked.

"No, but we've got a rehearsal scheduled tomorrow morning. We've been working up "There Will Never Be Another You" a little bit. We tried it at a fast clip, but it's coming along better at medium tempo."

"Don't you ever play anything new?" Hiroshi asked. He had little use for anything that wasn't right up to the moment and fashionable.

"Sure. You know we've got to."

"We'll come by tomorrow night," Ota said. "I mean Miyumi and I."

"Sounds like fun. Come by later on, and we'll go out afterwards."

"Can't do that. You forget that, unlike you boys, I have to get up early in the morning," Miyumi said regretfully.

"Well, come by early. We'll play some of our new stuff for you."

They talked and relaxed into the early afternoon as rain came down around the house in dark sheets. Sky offered to fix lunch, but they had to leave.

"We'll come to the club tomorrow night," Ota said as they stood by the door putting on their coats.

"I'll be looking for you. I hope it stops raining soon," Sky said. Miyumi smiled and looked pensively out into the street.

"Oh, I don't know. I kind of like it," she said.

"We'd better be going," Ota said as he walked out into the yard.

Miyumi paused for a moment before leaving. "Rain and

Monday. They belong together."

"It sure seems that way at times," Sky said. He waved good-bye, then watched as his three friends disappeared down the street, talking and huddling beneath their umbrellas.

The hard rain continued falling throughout most of Monday. The people of Yokohama moved through the streets and alleys of the city as it was washed in minor torrents down gutters and off rooftops. The days before Christmas were bleak, damp, and cold.

Chapter Twelve

Sayoko waited for Sky one night as he finished work at the Akabashi. She was in the company of a friend from the cabaret named Sumiko, who smiled shyly when Sayoko introduced her to Sky. She was shorter and thinner than Sayoko, and she had her shoulder-length hair brushed over from a right-hand part. She and Sayoko laughed and passed a bottle of whisky back and forth, trying to ward off the chill brought into the alley by the strong wind.

"Where do you feel like going?" Sayoko asked.

"It doesn't really matter. I'd like to get something to eat, maybe a few more drinks. How about you two?"

"What you said sounds fine. Let's go," Sayoko said, shivering and smiling.

They walked out to the street, caught a taxi, and headed for an all-night cafe that Sumiko suggested they try. The place was all but empty when they arrived, and they sat at a table in the back. The two girls ordered whisky, and Sky ordered fried rice and beer.

"Christmas will be here soon," Sumiko said.

"It won't be much longer now," Sky said with little feeling.

"Do you like to get presents?" Sayoko asked. She was dressed in black, and her skin was flushed from the cold. Her eyes were glittering in the half-light of the place. She

appeared to be tired but on edge, as though unable to relax.
"Never really thought about it, but I'll get one for you."
Sayoko brightened. "I'd like that."

They left the bar shortly after Sky had finished eating. The place was quiet and gloomy, and this fact hindered conversation and relaxation. They went to Sumiko's apartment, which was a short walk from the cafe. She had a small place on the fourth floor of her building. Some people passed them, on their way to work, as they made their way up the stairs. They sat around Sumiko's dining room table, drinking and talking as the sun came up, all but unnoticed in the overcast sky.

町 光 青

Sky woke up just before three o'clock that day. The afternoon had brought on a brighter sky, but he could see clouds beginning to move in once again. He had been sleeping in a large and comfortable futon in Sumiko's spare bedroom. Framed photographs of young women, including Sayoko, hung along one wall. Another wall was decorated with woodblock prints of old Tokyo's pleasure quarters. The room was small but pleasant, its one window hung with bright blue curtains.

Sky lay still and listened to Sayoko and Sumiko talking and laughing in the next room. He lay there lazily for a long time. He closed his eyes, knowing he should move, get up. He promised himself he'd stay in bed only five more minutes. He'd have to get up and get himself ready for work. He was a little behind schedule, but he didn't care. He took the five minutes and then got up and went into the dining room, where the girls' conversation continued. It was lively and filled with spontaneous emotion, fast-paced and entrancing. Sayoko and Sumiko paused briefly and smiled at him before going on with their talk. Sky walked over to the window and looked out. Children were playing in the street below, improvising games of their own. They were bundled up against the cold as played in the bitter wind of the alley.

"I'll be back soon. I'm going to fix some food," Sumiko said, getting up just after Sky sat down at the table. Sayoko looked at him with a wistful expression. She wore a faded pink robe and her hair was in appealing disarray. She put her hand on his arm and looked into his face. He noticed that she still looked sleepy, as if she hadn't shaken off recent dreams. She smiled and looked away toward the window.

"Did you sleep well?" she asked, her face still turned away from him.

"Very well, thanks. How about you?"

"Not bad."

Sumiko came back into the room carrying a platter filled with food. She had made omelets filled with rice and onions. She had also fixed a large pot of hot and fragrant tea. They started slowly in on their meal, giving compliments to Sumiko that caused her to smile and blush. They ate and talked as wind-bells made winter music outside the window.

A Town Where Lights Are Blue

Chapter Thirteen

Sky's quartet was sailing through a pre-Christmas evening and the Akabashi was crowded. Very few tables remained unoccupied, and people still continued to crowd in. The dance floor was jammed and the bar was doing steady business.

Sayoko came in early, not long into the second set. Sky went to wave to her until he saw that she wasn't alone. She was in the company of a young man. They held hands and appeared to be deep in intimate conversation. They left before the break song, and Sky put seeing her out of his mind for the time being.

Being Christmas Eve, the Akabashi stayed open later than usual, and it took some time to get the last of the keyed-up revelers out of the club. Mikio and Yasujiro left right after the last set, but Sky stayed behind after closing time along with Kenji. They sat on the edge of the stage, drinking beer and talking.

"It's Christmas Eve, Sky. Come on, let's go somewhere. There's going to be a lot of action in this old town tonight. We might as well get in on at least a little of it," Kenji said as he stood up. He stretched and rubbed his arms, then walked across the floor to get their coats.

Sky said nothing for a few moments and then looked around the now all-but-deserted club as though momentarily lost. "Let's make it," he said, standing up as Kenji walked over and handed him his coat and cane. They caught a taxi and rode to a club near the harbor that Kenji knew and recommended. Snow fell steadily as they made their way across the city, and Sky thought that the Christmas lights put up along the way looked more vulnerable than decorative or festive. Kenji gave their cab driver a small bottle of whisky, and the man accepted it gratefully.

町 光 青

Sky and Kenji entered the club around four thirty that morning. The place was big and crowded. The walls were done in schemes of bright pastel colors and an orchestra played on a large bandstand at the rear of the main room. Sky recognized the tune they played as the old theme of the Tommy Dorsey Big band, "Getting Sentimental Over You." They sounded competent if not overly enthusiastic, and he liked how their piano player made his presence felt in a way that was integral but unobtrusive. A number of couples in suits and formal clothes danced to the song, and they looked like they were having a good time.

"Don't you know anyplace smaller? I don't really like this kind of place very much," Sky said hesitantly, and Kenji smiled and shook his head.

"I've been in here lots of times. It's not as bad as you think. I've got to tell you, Sky, there are times when I'm convinced that a good time isn't in you. Anyway, it'll look better to you after a few drinks."

"I guess you're right," Sky said, sounding unconvinced.

"Come on. At least try to get into something like a good

mood. Look at all the women in here. On their own, and with class. Forget about that cabaret whore. It's not like she's in love with you or something."
"All right, all right. Whatever you say. It's pretty packed in here, but let's look around and see if we can find a table."

町 光 青

Sky felt an urge to leave the club as soon as they arrived. Kenji met a girl almost immediately. Sky didn't really expect to meet anyone, but he encountered in passing, among the crush and swirl of noisy bar patrons, an aging, embittered bargirl named Miyako. At first glance, the only thing she appeared to have in common with Sky was that she looked as isolated and as uncomfortable in the midst of all the noise and motion as he did.
"I don't really like foreigners very much," she said to him not long after she sat down at their table.
"Neither do I," he replied, and they lapsed into silence, drinking steadily and listening to the band.
They were still in the club at seven thirty that morning, and the place was at least as crowded and noisy as it had been when they first came in. It was as if the dancing and partying might go on forever. Sky and Kenji and the two women with them were very drunk by this time. The girl with Kenji, a tall young woman named Yumi, could barely keep her eyes open. In spite of this, however, she continued to order more drinks. Sky was surprised that she could still get them down, on through the night and into the morning. There had been a time when Miyako had fallen asleep leaning against Sky's shoulder, and he took care not to disturb her. In time she awoke

with a start and looked around, her eyes weary yet bright. She then left the table, and Sky was surprised when she returned some time later. She sat down and lit a cigarette. She appeared to have freshened up, but she still looked quite tired. She ordered another drink and then looked steadily at Sky.

"I'm thirty-six years old," she said, and he couldn't think of anything to say.

Miyako's voice had a hard edge, but he detected an undertone of gentleness just beneath it. They shared many rounds of drinks but only intermittent conversation throughout Christmas morning.

Sky began to feel tired, but Kenji seemed to never wear down. He found other girls to dance with after Yumi finally told him that she was too tired to do anything but drink. It was just past nine o'clock when he felt a tugging on his shoulder.

"Come on, John. It's time to go," Kenji was saying to him.

Sky had fallen asleep at the table and he looked slowly around, feeling disoriented, exhausted, and foolish. Kenji still looked wide-awake, but Yumi was virtually asleep on her feet as she leaned against his shoulder. Her eyes were glazed and she yawned expansively as she looked around the still-crowded room. Miyako looked at him in a way that seemed somewhat conspiratorial. He rubbed his eyes and got into his coat as Kenji handed him his cane. He got clumsily to his feet while looking at Miyako. She had just finished buttoning her coat and was slinging her black leather handbag over her shoulder. They moved slowly toward the door. It was just after nine twenty five.

町 光 青

    Miyako's house was small but neat and meticulously clean. The four of them sat around the kotatsu in her living room for a time until Kenji and Yumi got up and left.
    "Would you like something to eat?" Miyako asked, breaking the silence that hung in the air after the young people had gone.
    "I probably should, but no. No, thanks. I think I'm going have to go to sleep soon," he said, his voice thick with drink and fatigue. He was extremely tired and Miyako looked and sounded to be much the same.
    "Just relax here for a few moments. I'll go prepare the *futon*," she said and then left the room.

町 光 青

    "You know, I don't think I really like you very much, but I like being with you," Miyako told Sky later as they lay together in the darkness of her bedroom. He turned and looked at her profile, which at that moment was framed by the dark waves of her thick hair.
    "I think I can understand that."
    There was a distance between them. They didn't touch.

町 光 青

    Sky got up in the afternoon and went into Miyako's kitchen looking for something to relieve his roaring thirst.

A Town Where Lights Are Blue

He found some soft drinks and drank one avidly. He then felt slightly better, but by no means good. He went back into the living room and looked out the window. Snow was still falling, though not as heavily as before. He eased down at the kotatsu, lighting a cigarette without much interest in smoking it. He then walked into the bedroom and sat against the wall. He watched Miyako, who was still sleeping soundly. She gave the impression of losing much of her bitterness in sleep.

As Miyako slept, her long, coarse hair spread out on the pillow. Her face was almost plain yet intriguing. Her eyes were large and expressive, and her skin had a faint amber glow that was striking in certain kinds of light.

町 光 青

Sky looked up as he quickly and sheepishly came to the realization that he had fallen asleep while leaning against the wall. His back was sore, but his head no longer ached. He looked across the room at Miyako, who was sitting up. She brushed distractedly at her hair, which was extremely long. She put the brush away and pulled the comforter up to conceal her nakedness, looking both shy and indifferent about her current state. She seemed alert but she still looked half-asleep. She then smiled at him in a way that struck him as being both spontaneous and completely open.

"Please come here," she said, her voice still heavy with sleep. He walked unsteadily across the floor and sat down next to her.

"What time is it?" she asked.

"About four fifteen. Do you have a headache?" he asked

as he put his hand on her forehead. It felt warm.

She gently nodded her head. "Yes. A bad one. It hurts," she said, her voice trailing off.

"Do you need anything?" he asked, and she looked at him like she had something important to say. She shook her head and rubbed her eyes.

"You know, I woke up once earlier this afternoon. I was going to wake you up, but then I thought it would be better if I let you sleep. I don't even remember falling asleep again. I guess I just sort of dozed off sitting over there," he said, sounding amused.

"I probably shouldn't even tell you this, but I also watched you. At first I felt restless and I was going to make you get up and talk to me, but then I decided to let you sleep. You looked so peaceful," she said, her voice soft.

"Really?"

"Yes. Do you feel hungry?"

"Not really. How about you?"

"Well, I am a little bit hungry, but I don't want to eat yet," she said. She then rose slowly up and put her arms around him, causing him to feel awkward. She then kissed his cheek lightly and spoke to him in a slow, deliberate voice. "I was just now thinking that if neither of us like foreigners, then it must be all right for us, because that's exactly what we are."

"I guess there's nothing else for us to be," he said with mock solemnity, and she laughed.

Sky had expected Miyako's laughter to be bitter or ironic, but this wasn't the case. It was natural and unaffected and it put her in a new light.

"Did you have enough to drink on Christmas?" she then asked, giving the word "Christmas" a particularly biting sardonic emphasis.

"Just about."

"Maybe you and I are getting too old for this kind of thing."

"You could be right about that," he said. He kissed her, and she responded in a way that was tender yet almost fierce. She then looked openly at him and narrowed her eyes.

"I don't always like Americans very much, although I spend a lot of time around them. Japanese people often aren't very fond of me, because of what I do for a living. Do you like me?" Miyako asked, sounding breathless and pained.

"Yes."

"I see. And, it's a little strange, but I like you, too. I was interested in you from the first moment I saw you walking so alone through that crowded, noisy place. I have to tell you that such a feeling is unusual for me," she said, smiling and shaking her head as though genuinely confused. She then met his eyes and spoke again. "Maybe we just deserve each other?"

"That might be it," he replied, taking her hand as she laughed quietly.

町 光 青

Night came on quickly and the house was suffused with half-light and stillness. Miyako went out to buy some food for their dinner. Sky stayed behind, sitting in the living room and listening to selections from her disparate collection of record albums. The title of one of the pieces to which he listened that night caught his eye-a long piece for unaccompanied *koto* entitled "Water Music." As he sat in the stillness left in the air after the music's end, he felt that the sound of the music had perfectly matched the image evoked by its title. Miyako entered the house just after "Water Music" came to an end. Her face was flushed from the cold and her hair was wind-blown and wild.

"It's cold," she said.

Sky noticed that Miyako's behavior was different while she was in the comfortable familiarity of her house. Even her voice and movements were altered from what he observed of her behavior in public. As they sat at the *kotatsu* after eating dinner, she spoke to him in a serious tone about the reality of growing older.

"It won't be much longer. I know that. I can't be a bargirl forever. Nobody will be interested in being with an old woman. It's only logical," she said, her tone clinical and distant, but touched with sadness.

"You're not old, Miyako. You don't even look anywhere near your age. As for being a bargirl, there are other things you can do with your life. You don't have to be a bargirl."

"Yes I do," she said quickly, with a sense of finality that he found disturbing.

"Do you enjoy being a bargirl? Is it what you want to do?"

"Yes. No. I don't really know anymore," she said, and he was about to say something when she began speaking again in a slow and distant voice.

"It's all I know," she said, and her eyes looked far beyond him, into her past. He reached for her hands and held them tightly in the dark silence.

町 光 青

Miyako later showed Sky an album of photographs. It was filled mainly with pictures of her in the company of American servicemen. The pictures covered a span of eighteen years. Many of the photographs were dark and faded. Miyako was smiling in most of the pictures, but Sky thought that the smiles seldom went very far below the surface. She put the book away and looked at him. The wind blew tree branches against the window, and a faint trace of perfume drifted by him. He leaned back and sipped some of the tea she had prepared. She hesitated before speaking, as though carefully weighing her choice of words.

"I could be wrong about it, but I have a feeling about you. I'm not sure why, but I sense that you're not like other foreigners," she said slowly, thoughtfully. Her statement came across as being slightly matter-of-fact, and it surprised him.

"Is that good or bad?"

"Oh, it's good, as far as it goes, but it's mostly just different."

"Do you trust feelings like that when you get them?"

"For better or worse, I'm afraid that I do. At least most of the time," she said, and he wanted to make an immediate response. He paused, however, trying to sort out his thoughts into words that could accurately express the complexity of what he felt.

"Miyako, I want you to tell me something. If you're unhappy with your life here, and you seem to be, then why don't you move away to some other city or try to find some other kind of work?"

"I have to confess to you that it's something I think about now and then," she said slowly. She leaned forward at the *kotatsu*, brushing her hair back over her shoulders as she poured more tea, first for him, then for herself.

"Maybe I've got no right to give advice. It's your life. We've only just met. I can't explain how, but I think I understand the kind of feelings you're having about this. Of course, maybe I don't, not at all. Still, I think it's something that you ought to think about more than just now and then," he said.

Miyako was looking down, staring into her tea like she thought that answers might float by upon its surface. She looked around the room, at the plain brown walls and the barren neatness that spoke volumes about her inner being. She sat up straight, her eyes distant and filled with memories of the past and discomforting glimpses of the future. He sipped his tea and lit a cigarette, patiently waiting for a response, but prepared for the disappointment that her silence would bring. The wind brushed the window with a low and winter-laden sound, and the soft glow being emitted by the lamp on the kotatsu seemed pitiful and impotent in comparison to the cold light of the winter moon. She smiled, then looked serious, but she had nothing to say to him. At least not for the moment.

A Town Where Lights Are Blue

Chapter Fourteen

Sky was getting ready for work one afternoon when Sayoko stopped by. He was surprised when he opened the door and saw her there, smiling and shivering in the cold. She was carefully dressed, ready for work, and her eyes were lustrous in the cold winter air. She kicked off her shoes and came in, moving across the floor in quick lithe steps. She tossed her long dark coat carelessly across the chair and sat down at the *kotatsu*.

"Sorry, Sky. I missed seeing you on Christmas. I was busy," she said breathlessly.

"That doesn't matter. I saw you in the bar with your friend."

"Oh, him. He's nobody," she said in an offhand way, and Sky looked up suddenly and snapped his fingers.

"I have something for you," he said.

"Really?" Sayoko was smiling in anticipation. He left the room and returned momentarily carrying a small parcel wrapped in silver foil paper. Sayoko opened the package with care and smiled openly and warmly in a way that became her Christmas present to him. The box contained a pair of jade earrings.

"Hope you like them."

"I love them," she said, running her hand over the smooth green stones. "They're beautiful. Thank you, Sky."

"You're welcome."

"And now, I have something for you," she said, handing him a package.

"You didn't have to do this," Sky said, and Sayoko shook her head.

"You don't understand. I wanted to."

The package contained a record album of works by various *koto* masters, and he looked the titles over carefully.

"I hope you like it."

"I like it a lot. Listening to this will make me think of you," he said, and Sayoko frowned, then smiled.

"I'm going to work soon. You, too. Right?"

"I have to leave soon."

"I think about you sometimes, Sky," she said quietly, seriously. He was about to reply when she began speaking again. "Too much work for me these days. It's our busiest time. But maybe, in two days, I can come here. I'll wait for you after work. Is that all right?"

"Yes."

"I'll see you then. I have to go now. Two days, yes?"

"Two days," Sky said.

They kissed as he opened the door for her. She put on her shoes and turned quickly to wave, then ran across the darkening yard.

Chapter Fifteen

There were scattered snow flurries in Yokohama between Christmas and New Year's Day and the days and nights were bleak with a cold that was both bitter and unrelenting.

Sky stopped by a small restaurant near his house one night and bought some take-out food, having it in the back of his mind that it was a necessary thing to do. It was just after three in the morning when he arrived home, and he set out some food on the *kotatsu* in preparation for Sayoko's scheduled visit. He got a bottle of beer from the kitchen and placed a recording of a Beethoven piece for piano and cello on the turntable. He took a book over to the *kotatsu* and settled in to wait.

町 光 青

It was after four when he knew that Sayoko wasn't coming. He'd switched from Beethoven to Ike Quebec and had given up reading for drinking and smoking, taking time now and then to clear away the empties. He ate a little of the food, some rice and noodles, but there was still plenty left when Yasujiro and Ota dropped by around quarter to five. They had been drinking and unsuccessfully trying to meet girls. For all this, however, they were in good spirits.

"What're you doing sitting around here by yourself on a night like this? There's plenty of action in town tonight," Yasujiro said, helping himself to some cold rice. He ate hungrily, as though he had concentrated on drinking without eating.

"Just wasn't up for it this evening."

"Waiting for someone?" Ota said as he came in from the kitchen with three beers. He passed around the beer, then sat across from Sky. Wind blew tree branches against the window as a sudden series of gusts slammed through the alley. Sky shrugged his shoulders and said nothing. Ota spoke again without looking up.

"Omura Sayoko? The one from the cabaret?" he said, and Sky looked over at him and smiled, realizing that Ota would of course know.

"That's right."

Ota nodded and put together a bowl of noodles, still without looking up. "She won't be coming. Or, at least I don't think she will. I saw her downtown with a man old enough to be her grandfather. Come to think of it, maybe that's who it was," Ota said, his voice calm, uninflected, like a television newsman reporting a story from a far-away location.

"Yeah. Maybe," Sky said.

Yasujiro walked over and looked through the records. He looked them over carefully and smiled when he found one that looked interesting.

"Never heard this one," he said, setting the needle onto the LP. It was organ, alto saxophone, guitar, and drums. A blues ballad led off side one, filling the room in a solid but subtle way. Yasujiro walked back and sat at the *kotatsu*, poured some beer, and eased into the conversation going on in the space between the intermittent sounds of wind against glass and the saxophone stretching out in an solo filled with bitterness, depth, and raw feeling.

A Town Where Lights Are Blue

Chapter Sixteen

The new year passed without incident for Sky. He played with the quartet until four in the morning on New Year's Day and then went to a party with Mikio. He didn't leave until early that afternoon, feeling exhausted and drunk almost to the point of sobriety.

The earliest days of January were warmer and sunnier than the last days of the old year, but on the fifth of the month the city was hit by a violent winter storm that brought with it an onslaught of snow and icy wind.

It wasn't long after closing time at the Akabashi on the day that the winter storm broke when Sky, tired and walking unsteadily, entered a bar with Yasujiro. The place was large, noisy, and unknown to them both. It was set up with a number of small tables scattered across the floor with an area set off to one side for dancing. There was also a kind of loft or balcony along one wall.

They ordered beer and listened to the music from the jukebox, figuring to leave the place after one round. Sky saw Ota come into the smoke and haze of the bar in the company of a dark, slender young woman dressed in dark clothes. They crossed the room and climbed the stairs to the balcony, and Sky thought that he would let Ota settle in and then go up and speak to him before he left. It seemed to him that there were a number of people who looked out of place in the bar, but he couldn't have explained to anyone what that meant.

A group of men accompanied by a tall, tough-looking woman with long red hair came into the room and took a table near the jukebox. Sky didn't pay them much mind, because they appeared to belong in the place more than he did. Yasujiro had been dancing throughout most of their short stay, and he returned to the table after a song ended, smiling and sweating. He sat down and ordered another beer, saying that it would be his last. Sky nodded and continued looking at a series of crude-looking oil paintings along the near wall when he heard the first gunshots. He thought at first that it was an effect thrown into the song blaring through the room, but then he realized that it wasn't.

He heard a distinct crackle of what sounded like a high caliber pistol and then a startled, keening scream. He looked up and saw Ota standing beside the balcony railing, his white shirt marked by a diagonal sequence of jagged red splotches that spread slowly as Sky watched with unbelieving eyes. He moved quickly up and away from the table. Noise came from all sides of the room as he saw the dark, slender girl slump forward convulsively and fall over the rail and down across the smoky air.

It was a scene that was instantly and indelibly vivid to Sky, and one that he would see again many times after it took place, in waking hours and in fevered dreams. The girl, falling like she had been thrown, and yet oddly suspended, moving downward through the smoky, light-stabbed air. Her thick black hair flew out all around her until she landed hard and lay perfectly still at a jagged, disturbing angle.

He stood away from the table, his eyes on the form of the dead girl, her face betraying no signs of emotion. The noise inside the bar melded into a unified roar nonetheless made up of many discrete elements: music, screaming, splintering wood, hard shoes scraping on the floor. The quietly sinister energy of the place that had made Sky feel uneasy was now unleashed in a fury of unfocused violence. He saw Ota fall to the balcony floor, his shirt showing mostly red now. Someone had come out of the shadows in the rear of the place to stab one of the men who had come in with the red-haired woman. The man looked more startled than scared as he slumped down across the table, his hands grasping at the air. His assassin then turned his attention to the woman, stabbing her across her arms and throat as she went down in a chorus of gurgling screams, fighting the man off with surprising strength, her long legs flailing as she took him down with her.

Sky broke free of the daze through which he had been moving and saw someone coming up behind Yasujiro waving a broken bottle neck wildly and moving forward rapidly.

Moving quickly, Sky grabbed his cane off the table and started toward the man who held the broken bottle. As he moved forward, pushing Yasujiro out of the way, his glasses were knocked off by a violent blow from behind. They fell onto the floor and were crushed. He was only dimly aware of blurred forms rushing toward him as two searing sheets of pain exploded on either side of his chest. He was dizzy and sweat was pouring into his eyes, but he held steady and brought the cane down hard across the skull of the man carrying the broken bottle. He fell to the floor, pushed over and down by people rushing by, and the jagged bottle neck entered his leg above the knee. The last thing that Sky could recall being able to see was a splintered piece of his cane as it went hurtling across the frenzied, noise-filled air.

A Town Where Lights Are Blue

Chapter Seventeen

Sky could hear muffled voices gradually growing louder, and he became aware of movement. Although his vision was blurred, he was able to discern floating, ill-defined specks of light moving across his eyes, and in time he realized that he was sitting in the back of a car.

"What?" he said, his voice sounding strange and thin in his mouth.

"Don't talk." It was Kenji's voice.

"My glasses."

"Ruined. Gone. Forget about them."

"Yasujiro, you in here, too?" he asked. His voice seemed to be coming out of a deep place, and the few words he had spoken set his head to spinning.

"Yes."

"You all right?"

"I'm fine. Just be quiet now."

He looked around, but his eyes took in only a little, not much more than that he was sitting in the back seat of a car between Yasujiro and Kenji. He saw blurred forms wavering in front of him and after a while heard he Miyako's voice and then an unfamiliar male voice. He nodded and slumped back against the seat, realizing that Miyako was talking in a low voice to someone who had to be a taxi driver. Everything, everybody, around him was without form or substance, and the lights of the city flashed sporadically through the windows of the speeding car.

"Hell. What happened?" he asked at length, and there was a pause before Yasujiro answered.

"You've been hurt, badly. It's over now, whatever it was. I got you out of there. It's a lucky thing, too. People died in that place tonight, and I thought you were one of them. I mean, I thought you were gone. You were bleeding so much, and your breathing sounded all wrong. I never saw anything like that."

"What was it all about?" Sky asked hesitantly, and Yasujiro was a long time in answering.

"I think they were trying to kill Ota."

"Why did they shoot the girl?"

"I can't say. She probably just got in the way."

"Why Ota?"

"I guess it had something to do with one of those women he's always with. Maybe it was about the girl he was with tonight. I don't really know."

"What about Ota? Is he dead?"

"No. He was sent to a hospital in Tokyo. His condition is very bad, and I have to tell you that he may not make it."

"What about the girl?"

"She's dead. She died instantly. I'm sure of that," Yasujiro said, his voice flat and tired.

"You were out for some time. There was some trouble at the hospital. It's a little hard to explain. Kishida Miyako was there when we arrived, waiting for you," Kenji said, his voice sounding hollow and old.

"I don't understand," Sky said, and he could hear Yasujiro sighing heavily.

"Neither do I. I don't know how it happened, but she

was there. She just found out somehow. We're taking you to her house now. I won't lie to you, you're hurt pretty bad. She wants to take care of you, and I guess she can do a good job of it," Yasujiro said, then fell silent for a few moments before he began speaking again.

"You'll be out of things for a while, maybe a long time. I talked to Tsushima tonight, and he thinks you ought to go away, get out of Yokohama for a while. There might be some bad people mixed up in this, whatever it is, and they might be looking for you."

Sky wasn't able to make much sense of what Yasujiro had said, and, as he began to collapse into pain and exhaustion, it didn't seem to matter much. He felt himself slowly falling away even from the transitory light that slipped past his vision and into some dark place beyond it that was somehow familiar to him.

A Town Where Lights Are Blue

Chapter Eighteen

The passage of time didn't have much meaning for Sky in the days following the violent incident in the bar, and he wasn't always certain that it was going from past to present in the usual way. His blurred vision made it impossible to distinguish light from darkness, and days bled into nights beyond his knowing. He once thought that he saw Miyako sitting by the *kotatsu* in the next room, but he wasn't certain of this. He tried to separate the days and nights, but the light outside the window in the room where he lay always looked the same.

It was through a kind of mist that he was eventually able to actually realize the form of Miyako, as she stood by the window with her back to him. He could discern large snowflakes falling. The room felt cold but comfortable. He felt sore all over and it was only with some effort that he was able to raise himself up from the futon.

"Hell, I guess I'm alive," he muttered. His tongue felt thick, and he was light-headed. He could make out beard stubble and new scar tissue as he ran his hand over his face. Miyako turned around slowly and looked at him for a few moments before returning her gaze to the window and the snowfall.

"Yes, you're alive. That's something I've not always been certain of this week."

An odd, bittersweet smile crossed Miyako's face as she walked across the room to kneel by his side. She was wearing a *kimono* of pale blue, sitting with her hands folded in her lap. He noticed with concern that there were dark circles under her eyes and that she looked tired.

"How long?" he asked, and she was slow in responding.

"Some days," she said hesitantly. She then turned to him, her expression serious. "Tsushima says you need to leave as soon as you can. He believes that you'll be all right here for now, but not for much longer."

"I imagine he'd know, even if I don't. I guess I was in the wrong place at the wrong time," he said, regretting it. The expression covered a lot of ground and it could apply to many situations in many lives.

"It happens that way sometimes," Miyako said, her voice noncommittal yet melancholy.

"Just to some of us more than others. What about Ota? Any news from him?"

"I believe he's doing well, under the circumstances. The girl is dead. Cremated a few days ago. Did you know her well?"

"I didn't know her at all. I just happened to be there when she was killed."

A silence emerged between them as they both struggled for something to say.

"You've been sleeping for so long. Aren't you hungry now?"

"Not really, but I'd appreciate a drink of water," Sky said. Miyako nodded and left the room. She returned shortly carrying a large glass filled with water and ice.

"Thanks," he said, and then drained half the glass. He

then sipped a little more and set the glass down on the table alongside the futon.

"Better?" she asked.

"Much."

"Sky, I don't know about you sometimes. Are you all right? How do you feel now?" Miyako said, sounding uncomfortable. She fought to keep concern out of her voice but ultimately failed. Sky was confused about why she might be concerned about him. He had been hurt before, much worse than this. Her concern seemed an unlikely part of her character, until he realized that he hardly knew anything about her. He didn't know where she was from, if she had any family, what kind of music she liked. He knew that, like him, she liked to drink, and, like him, she worked in a bar. He wanted to know more, but for the moment he was gratified that, for whatever reason, she was worried about him. It was something new to him.

"I'm all right," he said, and Miyako nodded, her face away from him.

"I brought your other glasses from your house, and your other cane. The one that you liked to use, the one with the Indian markings, is gone now. There's also a letter that one of your friends from the band brought by. Do you want to read it now?"

"No, thanks. I'll take a look at it later."

The house shook in the wind as night settled down upon it. Miyako got up silently and left the room. Sky opened and read the letter that had been brought to the house by Mikio. It was from Sayoko. She was visiting relatives in Tokyo and wanted to see him when he went there to visit Ota. She gave him a street address where they could meet and a tentative time. It seemed unlikely that she would ever keep such an appointment, but he realized, as in the case of Miyako, that he didn't know very much about Sayoko.

Miyako came back into the bedroom and stretched out on the *tatami* next to the *futon*. He raised up and looked over at her, then lay back down. He reached out and touched her arm. It felt cool and smooth. Dry snowflakes blew sporadically against the window. They said nothing for a time, until she crossed the floor and lay alongside him. He reached over and ran his hand through her waist-length hair.

Miyako stood up, paused for a moment as though deep in thought, and then began removing her *kimono*, placing it into the closet at the end of this complex process. She walked back across the room as stippled silver light coming in through the window created shifting patterns of light and darkness across her skin. She moved the comforter aside and moved in close to him. She lay on her stomach, and he began stroking her long, coarse, deeply black hair.

"I don't want you to go, but I know that it can't be helped," she said, and he nodded. She was smiling at him, looking tired. As he continued stroking her hair, he came upon a sudden burst of color that had up until that moment been obscured by the length and thickness of her hair. It was a chrysanthemum tattooed on her back, just beneath her right shoulder, with a line of *kanji* script running vertically to the left of the blossom, the colors of which were softly vivid against the pallor of her skin.

"Tell me about this," he said wonderingly, softly rubbing her back in the area of the tattoo, and she rolled over, smiling in a way that suggested shyness, and it was clear that he had embarrassed her.

"All right, I will. I guess I was hoping you'd never notice it, but that never seemed likely. I feel a little silly about it, and I sometimes forget about its being there. I got it years ago, in Yokosuka. I had just turned nineteen and I went into a place with some of my girlfriends. We were all young, and pretty drunk at the time. I didn't really have the intention of getting one, but then they all started to tease me, and I gave in. We went back to my apartment after that and sat up drinking all night, listening to ballads, laughing, and cursing the pain."

"Do you ever regret having it?"

"Now and then, but not often. Do you understand the characters?"

"Not all of them," he replied, sounding somewhat embarrassed himself.

"It's mostly just my name, and some other things that are no longer important to me," she said, noticing that his eyes didn't appear to be focused on anything close at hand.

"I could do that," he then said.

"Do what?"

"Have your name tattooed on me."

"You'd want to do that?"

"Maybe."

"Maybe you already have," she said, kissing his hand as she took it into both of hers and he looked at her like someone coming out of a deep and dream-plagued sleep. He was very tired, and he ached all over. Still, for all that, he felt at peace, and warm with a feeling he'd never experienced before.

"I don't want to go away. If I stayed here long enough, I might get to liking you or something, and then I wouldn't know what to do about it," Sky said, the words coming slowly in this failed attempt at a joke, negated by the truth it contained. Miyako smiled languidly, looking tired and yet ready to meet any challenge. She ran a finger slowly down his cheek, down the dark stubble and the new scars.

"I've always had bad luck, all my life, and then I meet you and it only gets worse. Maybe I should've left you to your problems at the hospital," she said, and then rose up quickly and kissed him with deep tenderness and looked into his eyes with an expression of raw sorrow.

"I'm sorry. I didn't mean that. I always say things like that when I mean something else."

"I understand. I do the same thing. I'd like to stay here with you, but that's not going to happen. At least not now."

"But maybe later?" she said, her voice low, hardly more than a whisper.

"Later, one way or the other. I'm going to miss you," he said, and she looked up, almost smiling. She looked like she was going to speak, but she said nothing.

Miyako was almost asleep now. Her hair fanned out across the pillow, a deep ebony shawl. She reached over and took his hand as the night moved deeper into the house and pulled them into sleep.

町 光 青

Sky left Yokohama that morning, not knowing when or if he'd be back. Miyako chose not to see him off at the station, preferring to say her words of parting there at the house. The last image that he had of her as he walked away was one of silence and beauty, as she knelt by the *kotatsu* with the smoke from a hastily lit and instantly forgotten cigarette curling up past her downcast head.

Chapter Nineteen

Sky didn't feel at ease while in Tokyo, and for some reason the feeling that he had for Japan excluded the capital city, as though it gave off an air of stifling activity in which he couldn't comfortably exist.

Ota was staying at a large hospital located in the center of the city and Sky arrived there shortly past noon. He spoke with the doctor in charge of Ota's case, who told him that his condition was still serious but improving. He'd still require considerable care and he wouldn't be able to leave the hospital for some time to come.

Ota's room was on the third floor and Sky found it without difficulty. Ota shared the room with an extremely old man who was in serious condition and near death. The walls of the room were stark white and the lighting was impersonal and harsh. The whole atmosphere of the room was pervaded with the antiseptic smell that Sky had always associated with hospitals. He walked across the room and pulled a wooden straight-backed chair alongside the bed. Ota was awake, looking out the window, although there didn't appear to be much to see.

Ota lay on his back surrounded by a profusion of tubes and wires and bottles and flowers. He looked both feverish and chilled, and his skin had a waxy, sallow appearance that was alarming to see. He looked smaller, and much older, than

Sky remembered him being. Sky sat beside the bed for several moments before he could bring himself to speak.

"How are you getting along?" he asked, and there was a long pause before he received a response. The old man on the other side of the room moaned softly in pain. Winter sunlight spilled into the room, but it was lacking in appreciable warmth. When Ota finally spoke, his voice was tired and strained.

"The pain drifts in and out, but I think I'm going to make it now."

"I have no doubt about that. I had quite a talk with your doctor downstairs. He's a good man. I liked him right off. He's got to be one of their best. It's bad, but you're going to be okay."

"If you say so."

"Have you had many visitors?"

"Hiroshi was here. He's gone now, down to Osaka. He's appearing in another one of those awful science fiction movies."

"Another one of those? He must have made fifty of them by now. Say, I saw Miyumi before I left. She sends you her best. She'll probably be up here in a day or two. She said she was coming to see you," Sky said, and Ota looked up with interest, almost smiling.

"You're sure she said that?"

"Hey, I'm not lying. I ran into her one day and we talked about you. She really misses you. You can be sure about that." Ota nodded, but Sky was unable to read any meaning in his blank expression.

"Who's playing piano at the Akabashi now?"

"They're working as a trio. They've done it before. Tsushima told me to take some time off to get my strength

back."
"Sounds like a good idea. How're you feeling now? Still pretty sore?"
"Just a little. It isn't bad. Miss Kishida did a good job of looking after me in my convalescence," Sky replied, and Ota smiled tiredly.
"Oh, yes. I'd almost forgotten about her. She's a strange one, but then so are you. Keep your eyes on her. Don't let her get away."
"I'll take your advice," Sky said, glancing at his watch. "Did you happen to bring any cigarettes along?"
"I did, but you can't do anything like that. Not yet."
"Not just one?"
"Sorry, but I've got to show a little common sense now and then, even it does give people the wrong impression of me," Sky said, as Ota smiled and shook his head. Sky realized that he should leave.
"Ota, I'd like to stay longer, but your doctor told me he could only authorize a short visit. You need your rest. I'll be by tomorrow."
"I'll be glad to see you if you come, but I'll understand if you don't. I'll know why," Ota said. He reached out his hand and Sky gently shook it. He was no longer able to speak. The notion of Ota lying there helpless and far from totally recovered wasn't in the natural order of things. He wanted to ask questions, to try to find out about what happened the night when Ota got shot and the girl got killed, but he decided to put it off. Maybe Ota didn't want to talk about it, or maybe he didn't know any more about what happened than Sky did. Maybe it was something as simple as jealousy or hatred. Ota was his closest friend, but there were probably parts of his life that Sky knew nothing about. What happened

in the bar that night could have been something that had been a long time in coming, or it could have been a totally random act of violence. He pushed his chair away, and it scraped loudly across the tile floor, its sudden noise like an explosion blossoming in the deep silence. He walked slowly out of the room and through the busy corridor on his way to the elevator, but he was actually in a hurry to leave.

Chapter Twenty

Sky rode across Tokyo in a taxi to the street address that Sayoko had mentioned in her letter, which turned out to be an intersection of two busy streets in the heart of the Ginza. He didn't have to wait there long before he saw her coming down the street. She was dressed in fashionable western clothes, and she was smiling brightly and apparently oblivious of the bitter cold. She took his arm and kissed his cheek, and they began walking down the street. She spoke to him in a bright, breathless voice that spilled out of her in an avalanche of restless energy.

"How are you? Are you all right? Do you need anything? You look so worn out," she said, the questions and the statement all coming out as one staccato block of unstressed syllables.

"I'm all right, thanks. You don't have to worry about me. I'm tougher than people give me credit for. I don't feel so bad now. How've you been? You look beautiful," he said, and she cocked her head to one side and smiled openly, then paused for a moment as though recharging her energy source.

"I've been well, thank you. What about your friend? What about Ota? I heard that it was very bad for him."

"It was, but I think he's coming out of it all right, just maybe kind of slowly. I guess it's going to take some time."

"I see."

"Do you think you could go by the hospital and visit him sometime? I know you don't really know him, but I do. He's down right now, and I know he'd be pleased by a visit from you."

"I'll go by. I'll take him a present."

"I'm sure that just seeing you would be enough. When're you going back to Yokohama?"

"In two more days. What about you, Sky? When will you go away?"

"Very soon. Most likely tomorrow."

"Have you decided where you're going?"

"Yes, I have. I'm going to Karatsu," he said, and Sayoko looked startled. She backed away from him, jostling into passersby, her eyes widening in disbelief.

"To Karatsu? Kyushu? Why there? There's nothing there. No people," she said, making the southern city sound like an uninhabited void, which he knew wasn't the case.

"It's not quite that way. Anyway, I don't think it'll be as barren as you make it sound," he said. Sayoko looked thoughtful but unconvinced.

"I suppose that might be true. Still, I would've thought that, if you're going in that direction anyway, Kumamoto would make a better choice," she said, and Sky nodded, conjuring up an image of that Kyushu city in the mountains, with the imposing volcano called Mount Aso close at hand.

"That makes sense, but it's too far away from the sea to suit me," he said, and she nodded and looked serious.

"I hadn't thought of that," she said. They fell silent, then resumed walking through the crowd moving like a strong current along the sidewalk, until Sayoko spoke again.

"How do you like Tokyo?"

"I guess it's all right. I just feel kind of lost here."

"It's not the same as Yokohama for you, is it?" she asked, an undercurrent of warmth flowing beneath her matter-of-fact tone.

"Not very much, no."

"Can you stop by and visit me later on?"

"I could probably come by later, in the evening. Where are you staying?" he said, and he was taken off guard when she told him that she had taken a room in a well-known hotel that, as far as he knew, catered mainly to foreigners.

"I see. I'll be by later on today."

"Good. John, do you need any money to tide you over, or anything else before you go away?"

"No, but thanks for offering. I've got quite a bit set by, and I borrowed some from Tsushima. I plan to live simply when I get to where I'm going. I'll make out all right," he replied. She nodded but looked worried.

"If you're certain. I'd like to talk some more, but I have to leave now. I've got to visit my aunt. She's an old lady, very old-style Japanese. She'll be upset if I don't see her."

"Of course she will. You get on over there and visit her."

"Don't forget to come by tonight," Sayoko said, more question than imperative.

"I'll be there."

"Please smile," she said, and the noise and motion surrounding him faded for a few moments. Sayoko frowned briefly before a smile emerged slowly and dazzlingly. He was distracted, tired, and not completely free of pain, but he couldn't keep himself from smiling. Sayoko nodded, looking pleased, having accomplished something that was important to her. Sky clutched her hand, its smooth, fine-boned beauty giving him a sense of something that was both molten and refreshingly cool. Sky thought that she was very close to him at that moment, like a confidante, like family, like something that had no easy explanation. He reassured her about his visit, and she said good-bye and stepped suddenly and fluidly out into the traffic-choked street, the cars appearing to suspend their motion, stress, and anger as she crossed to the other side like she was fording a cool and shallow stream.

Chapter Twenty-One

Sky felt out of place as he walked across the hotel lobby. Most of the people who moved throughout the crowded space were middle-aged and well-dressed Americans. His bad leg was causing him more pain than usual and his chest felt sore. His eyes were red from the beer that he had drunk earlier with his cheap meal of rice and noodles in a sidewalk stall. Some of the hotel patrons glanced at him with a superficially genteel mixture of disdain and curiosity, but no one spoke to him.

He got the number of Sayoko's room from the desk clerk, a well-groomed and polite young man who seemed reluctant to pass on the information. Her room was on the sixth floor and the elevator was empty except for him as he rode up. He knocked on the door and heard her voice from inside, telling him in a gentle tone to come in.

"It's nice to see you. Is it cold out tonight?"

"It's getting to be, but it's not too bad so far."

Sayoko was wearing a dark green robe. She was brushing her hair and singing an old Japanese song. There was a cigarette burning in an ashtray among the many containers of cosmetics and pills that were laid out in a kind of a chaotic precision across the dressing table where she sat. Aside from the clutter of the dressing table, the room was neat and well-ordered. All of her clothes were put away and her jewelry was carefully arranged on a nightstand next to the large western-style bed.

"I could have some food sent up if you like. Unless you'd rather go out for dinner."

"No, thanks. Don't bother. I had something not long ago. But, please, go ahead and order something if you're hungry," he said. He sat in a chair in the center of the room, then spoke again. "By the way, when did you start smoking?"

"Oh, that. It's nothing. I don't do it all the time. Just now and then."

"You shouldn't do it at all," he said sternly, and she smiled like she was pleased by his remark.

"You do it," she said defensively, her voice very soft.

"You don't have to do the bad things I do just because I do them."

"I'm sorry. I didn't know you felt so strongly about it. I won't do it anymore."

She went back to brushing her hair and humming the old song, and he got up from the chair and crossed the room. He lay down on the bed, suddenly feeling tired and sore. He sat up quickly, feeling self-conscious, and walked back and sat in the chair. Sayoko got up from the dressing table and walked across the room. She knelt alongside the chair with her hands resting on one of its arms.

"You look so lovely tonight. You know, I've got to say it. I don't understand why you want somebody like me around," he said, and she frowned, then smiled, looking surprised.

"You really don't understand? You should know. Why shouldn't I like you?" she asked, and Sky nodded and fumbled for his cigarettes. He looked down, smiled, and put them away. He wiped sweat from his forehead and stretched out his damaged leg as best he could.

Sayoko's thick hair fell around the soft lines and angles of her face. She was still smiling, but he noticed that her beauty was underscored with a kind of resigned weariness that had always been hidden up until this time by things like makeup, dark bar lighting, or the glow of alcohol. The front of her robe had come open slightly and he could see that she was wearing a star-shaped pendant on a silver chain. He thought that it highlighted the golden quality of her skin quite well. She broke off her humming and looked up.

"Would you like to look at some pictures?"

"Of you?"

"Of me, of my mother, lots of people."

"Sure. I'd be interested in that."

She took a large, battered tan envelope from her purse and began showing him a number of photographs: Sayoko as a child, as an awkward but by no means unlovely teenager, as a young woman with familiar scenes of Yokohama often in the background. There were also several pictures of her mother, who impressed Sky as being exceptionally beautiful in a way that was in no way conventional, in the Japanese sense of the term or any other. She seemed willowy, ethereal, yet very strong. She then showed him an old and tattered photograph of a young black man in a US Army dress uniform. The man wore the crossed-rifle insignia of the infantry and he had the chevrons of a staff sergeant. He wore a blue presidential citation above the right pocket of his Eisenhower jacket, and there were three rows of ribbons topped by the silver and blue Combat Infantryman's Badge over the left.

"This is my father, Sky-Chan," she said wistfully, sadly, and he was initially startled. He looked first at the photo, then at Sayoko, as she continued to speak.

"He fought in the Pacific War, but your army wouldn't let black soldiers fight at that time. Still, he saw great battles. The Philippines, Peleliu, and he drove a kind of landing boat at the big fight at Iwo Jima. He came to Japan during the occupation. He got a medal for that. See? There's the ribbon for it. He met my mother during that time. He was a strong man, and he had seen war, but he was very kind to my mother. Japan was ruined then, nothing like it is now. He learned to speak Japanese, and my mother spoke good English, so they could always talk easily. They shared many things, happiness and bad times, love and hatred, joy and disease. Many people were sick in Japan when the war ended. But their love grew, like a flower growing in a wasteland. Then, when the war broke out in Korea, he was in one of the first groups to go."

"25th Division," Sky said, noticing the red and yellow 'tropic lightning' patch on her father's right sleeve, the mark of a combat veteran.

Sayoko nodded and then continued. "He went to Korea when I was little. About a year old. He came back once, on leave, as many of the soldiers did, and then he returned to the war. He didn't come back again. He was killed at a place called Munsan-Ni. Do you know that place, Sky?" she asked softly, and he thought for a few moments, but he couldn't recall having ever heard of the place. It wasn't surprising. Unlike the big battles of earlier wars, most of the major campaigns of the Korean War were unknown to many Americans, as were the places in Vietnam where he had seen good soldiers fight and die, places like Tan Tru, Go Cong, Long An, and some places that didn't have any name at all.

"I'm not familiar with it," Sky said, and Sayoko looked

up, her eyes shining with tears, looking overwhelmingly beautiful and profoundly exhausted. He didn't know what to say, so he brought out his wallet and showed her one of the few surviving photographs of his mother. The snapshot was old, faded, and ripped, but these less than pristine conditions couldn't diminish the beauty the old picture contained. Sky's mother was in the first bloom of young womanhood, peaceful yet self-assured, if in what seemed to be a shy and self-deprecating way, as though she found it hard to take her considerable loveliness seriously. Her long black hair was shining as a breeze lifted it away from her face, and her smile was radiant against a background of approaching prairie nightfall. Sayoko's eyes widened as she looked intently at the picture.

"Hey, Sky, you're making me kind of jealous. You never told me about any beautiful girlfriends like this," she said quietly, and she spoke again before he had a chance to respond. "Why would you want to come to Japan when you've got a pretty girl like this at home?"

"That's not a girlfriend, Sayoko. She's my mother."

"She's from Hawaii?"

"No. She was born and brought up in Montana, back in America. She's an Indian. Well, part Indian, really. But a big enough part to cause problems for her, I guess."

"From India?" Sayoko said.

"No. An American Indian. The story goes that Christopher Columbus landed in what was then called "the New World" and thought he was in India. He called the native people Indians. The name stuck," he said, and Sayoko glanced up, looking serious and thoughtful.

"Do you ever hear from her?" she asked tenderly, looking at him, brushing strands of hair and the remains of tears from her face.

"No. She died a long time ago, Sayoko," he said, putting the picture away. It looked like she was now the one at a loss for words, but she was simply taking her time, searching for the right thing to say. A warm, gentle light came into her eyes when she found it. She took his hand and he stood up. He held her close until she broke away slowly and walked over to turn off the lights.

"Come on, please. We don't have a lot of time. You're going to Kyushu, a long way from here, and this Japanese lady wants to share her love with you. Because we may never have another chance after tonight."

Soft winter moonlight came into the room filtered through pale translucent curtains and began to merge with the ensuing silence and the slow darkening of the room in places where light couldn't find its way.

Chapter Twenty-Two

Sky stood with Sayoko among the people who had crowded onto the platform to wait for the southbound train. A light snow was falling and the air had begun to get colder.

"Maybe you can sleep on the way, get some rest," Sayoko said.

"That's not a bad idea. Thanks for the books. They'll help pass the time."

"You're welcome. Please write to me, when you have a chance. You can send letters to my home in Yokohama. You don't have to worry about anything," she said. She was trying to be bright and cheerful, but her voice sounded diminished and unsure.

"I promise to write, but I've got to tell you that I've never been much of a correspondent."

"I understand. Just try to write a little, if you can find time," she said. They were standing apart from one another, feeling awkward and self-conscious in the pale winter light. He was glad to see her finally smile in a way that made her seem ageless and filled with the secrets of a difficult but wondrous life.

"Time to leave now. Don't stay around here much longer. The air's turning colder."

"I'm going soon. Take it easy, Sky."

They embraced, but only for a brief moment before he

pulled away. He took his suitcase and walked toward the train, taking his place in the line of passengers waiting to board. He then heard her call his name, and he turned to see her, waving and smiling in spite of the tears that crossed her cheeks.

"Sky, take care of yourself, okay?"

"I will. You do the same, Sayoko."

The train pulled away down the tracks, moving slowly at first, and he glanced back and saw her look down, then up again, still smiling. He kept his eyes on her as her image continued to recede, until at last he could no longer see her at all.

Chapter Twenty-Three

The train that Sky rode arrived in Karatsu early in the morning. It was raining at the time, but the sky looked to be clearing. The rain didn't last long, but a strong wind was blowing in from the ocean, and he could see some clouds forming and thickening far out across the sky to the east. He walked the streets of Karatsu with no particular destination in mind, noticing that it was getting colder. In time he found an inexpensive, old-style inn near the ocean where he decided to spend his stay.

The inn where he stayed was owned and operated by an energetic middle-aged woman named Mrs. Igawa. She was initially, if not unpleasantly, surprised by the prospect of having an American staying at her hotel. Sky's room was small and sparsely furnished. It had a window on one side that faced the sea and another facing Karatsu castle, which was located on a hill not far from the inn.

Sky took a walk through the city shortly after unpacking in an attempt to get something of a feel for the place. He walked up the hill to the castle and stayed there for some time before walking back down the hill, across a nearby bridge, and into the main part of Karatsu. He was able to discern little, if any, American influence in the city, despite its proximity to Fukuoka to the north and Sasebo to the south, cities that contained large American military installations either in or near them. He thought that he detected a kind of spontaneous energy flaring into life as the daylight began to fade. The lights that began coming up around him as he walked along seemed to be linked to an undeniable vitality that was as intriguing as it was unfamiliar.

Sky stopped for awhile in a small bar, a crowded working-class place presided over by two young female bartenders. He exchanged rounds with other patrons during his time there. Some of them told him stories of their lives working on fishing boats or in shops. The place was small, noisy, and overall rambunctious but congenial. It was also inexpensive enough to suit his modest budget. The stories he listened to were interesting, and he stayed on until almost midnight, which he realized was later than he should have. He then resigned to live a structured and almost monastic life while in Karatsu, even if doing that would take a great deal of effort on his part. As he walked toward the inn at the end of his first day in this unknown new city, the tension that he had felt initially eased, although he realized that it would probably resurface in the morning, when the alcohol warmth had faded. It began to snow as he walked cold and quiet streets on his way back to Mrs. Igawa's pleasant little inn.

Chapter Twenty-Four

Sky's stay in Karatsu gave him the illusion of being suspended in time as days passed into nights in a sequence of superficial regularity. He did little when he first arrived in the city. However, as time passed, he began to get out more and in doing so developed something of an affinity for the place. He got to know a few people during his stay, mostly other patrons at the inn or regulars at the little bar where he went on his first night in the city. He got to know Mrs. Igawa quite well. She was a widow in her late forties. She had opened the inn shortly after her husband's death and discovered that she had a natural gift for the hotel business. She had two daughters-Kazumi, who was thirteen, and Momoko, who was two years younger. Sky spent some of his time in Karatsu teaching the girls how to play a few songs on the old piano their mother owned. The girls were bright and enthusiastic and they learned quickly. They were proud of their musical accomplishments, and they were invariably eager to share any new songs with their mother. She was delighted when they would surprise her by playing an old Japanese folk melody, fragments of Sky's favorite Mozart concerto (his first), a Memphis soul tune, or some fractured chords from a Fats Waller song. Sky was pleased with their progress, but he knew that his skills as a teacher were limited. He encouraged the girls to keep up their lessons in a more serious way, meaning that they find a real music teacher. At first they were reluctant, because they liked his informal style of instruction, but in time they saw the wisdom of his advice, and they were eager to keep learning. Mrs. Igawa didn't know of any teachers, but she knew a lot of people in Karatsu and felt certain that she'd find someone suitable.

Sky also spent time telling Mrs. Igawa and her daughters some of the stories and legends that his mother and uncle had passed on to him while he was growing up. These storytelling sessions usually took place on rainy winter evenings in Mrs. Igawa's comfortable western-style living room. She usually made tea and rice cakes for these activities, and Sky, who was reluctant at first, came to enjoy these times very much. Kazumi, Momoko, and their mother made a good audience, and occasionally one of the stories put them in mind of old Japanese tales, which they shared with him. The stories that Sky told were tales based on Crow legends, matter-of-fact yet esoteric, at least to him, and often subtly charged with a sense of mystery and wonder. In return, Mrs. Igawa helped him with his *kanji* and *kana*, whereas Kazumi and Momoko helped him expand his Japanese vocabulary. To Sky, it seemed like an excellent arrangement.

One of the things that Sky most enjoyed doing while in Karatsu was going to films with Kazumi and Momoko. They saw both Japanese and American films covering a wide range of subjects. He saw Japanese period films and American westerns, comedies, and many other kinds of pictures. The first film he took them to see was actually an Italian picture. It had been filmed in Spain by an Italian director and featured American actors in leading roles. This whole idea struck Sky as humorous. He later heard this kind of film referred to as a "Spaghetti Western," which seemed apt. Kazumi, Momoko, and their mother all laughed heartily when he passed this term on to them.

He received a few letters from Sayoko and one from Yasujiro telling him, among other things, that business at the Akabashi had been steady and that the absence of his piano in the group was sorely missed. They were working as a trio and doing fairly well. He also received a couple of short notes from Tsushima. Sky was surprised to get these, because he had a reputation as a terrible correspondent who preferred using the telephone to communicate messages over distances. Tsushima's letters were off-hand yet cryptic, and Sky was initially shocked to realize how little he knew about his boss, a man he had thought he knew well. Tsushima mentioned in the last of his letters that the time when Sky could safely return to Yokohama wasn't far off, saying that things were returning to normal, although Sky didn't really know what that might mean.

Sayoko's letters were usually short and suffused with energy, giving the impression that they had been written in haste, but not without feeling and warmth. He thought that they were typical of her, if anything was really typical of her. Her letters were always brief, but never indifferent or glib. As in her speech, her letters reflected what was really on her mind. She said and wrote what she felt.

He received one letter from Miyako, a long, rambling effort that had apparently been picked up and put down a number of times before its completion, as if she had picked it up and worked on it when she had the sufficient time and energy to do so.

Miyako's letter was confessional, introspective, more

about her than to him. At first Sky thought that it was an odd concept for a letter, until he began to realize that she was using it to convey important things that she couldn't share with anyone other than him. It was filled with references to the dread induced by her upcoming birthday and musings about suicide that suggested she had both an intense fear of it and a fascination with it, and long-silent truths occasionally surfaced beneath her words. She was drinking more than usual, and her drinking had always been heavy. The emptiness and bitterness of her past had taken deep root in her, and she had recently taken to using pills to help her sleep, often borrowing them from some of the younger bargirls in her circle, something she had never done before. Her letter was more than anything else characterized by a singular self-criticism thoroughly devoid of either self-pity or melodrama. She was just passing on information. The letter wasn't always easy for Sky to read, because, even when discussing the most sensitive or disturbing matters, Miyako's tone was generally unemotional, although he knew this had to be only what was on the surface. The truths beneath her almost clinical tone couldn't be denied or suppressed. The letter ended abruptly and was signed simply: "Your Friend, Miyako."

As he sat in the silence of his room, looking out at the ocean, Sky thought about the bleak insights that resonated throughout Miyako's letter. He reread it many times, always finding something he had missed in previous readings. He sat in the semi-darkness of his room with night coming on, thinking that the winter had gone on very long and was still far from over. His winter thoughts had little to do with sub-freezing temperatures or snowfall at evening, but with the deep chill that the cold, confessional tone of

Miyako's words had put into his body and spirit. It was a chill that no fire, no warmth, could ever subdue. Feeling tired but restless, he got up and left the inn. He walked to the bridge beneath the castle, seeing many people as he passed along, but thinking only of Miyako, in the way she had materialized while he was reading her letter. He stopped and looked toward the city. Karatsu, its lights dim yet insistent through fog and broken snow, reminded him for a moment of Yokohama. He then took another look, gazing into the distance where city lights receded into darkness, and he saw that it wasn't really like Yokohama at all.

A Town Where Lights Are Blue

Chapter Twenty-Five

Sky kept a low profile during most of his stay in Karatsu. He was conscious of his limited budget made up of his savings, his salary advance from Tsushima, and the army disability payments that he had sent to him. He practiced on Mrs. Igawa's piano every day. He also read a great deal and went to movies frequently. The time that he most enjoyed was that which he was able to spend with Mrs. Igawa and her daughters. They made him feel at home during the time he spent living at the inn, a feeling that wasn't familiar to him. He changed his schedule from the one that he maintained while in Yokohama and usually went to sleep early. As the time drew near for him to leave the city, he was aware of things he'd miss, but he was nonetheless anxious to go.

When the day came for Sky to leave Karatsu, he woke up early with a bad hangover, having gone out drinking the night before. Except for his first night in the city, it was his only example of serious drinking during his stay there. He felt disoriented and sore as he finished packing and got ready to leave. Mrs. Igawa prepared a big breakfast for him, a combination of both Japanese and American food. He ate it in her kitchen, feeling saddened by his having to leave. He'd miss the kindly innkeeper, and he'd also miss Kazumi and Momoko. They were kind, plainspoken, honest people, and the simplicity of their lives had left its mark on him in a way that he couldn't fully understand. He seldom felt at ease around people, but this hadn't been the case while staying at the inn.

Mrs. Igawa, Kazumi, and Momoko accompanied him to the station. They spoke with him on the platform and loaded him down with souvenirs, magazines, and food. He invited them to visit him in Yokohama. The girls had sounded like they were eager for such a reunion, but Sky knew that Mrs. Igawa's life kept her too busy to do much traveling. They left the station before his train departed, and he was glad for this. The parting was difficult enough as it was.

The trip back to Yokohama was long, uncomfortable, and uneventful. He looked through the magazines he'd been given and got his meals from vendors who crowded the platforms during stopovers in various towns and villages. He tried to sleep, but his hangover caused him just enough discomfort to make this impossible.

Chapter Twenty-Six

Sky's train arrived in Yokohama early in the morning. He got his suitcase and packages and left the train, surprised to notice that there were only a few people other than himself who were disembarking. Most of the people he passed as he went through the station looked like he felt-tired and not quite awake. He walked wearily through an underground corridor and up into the main level of the station. Finding no taxis waiting outside, he began to walk away. He walked a few blocks before he was able to flag down a passing cab, and he rode toward his house as a drizzling rain began to fall.

It was nearly dawn and the traffic was sparse. It didn't look like a scene typical of Yokohama, at least not the one that Sky knew. The dead neon outside the nightclubs and bars looked tawdry and uninviting in a way he had never noticed before. He arrived home just as the rain began to fall harder, and he saw Miyako sitting alone on the steps. She was huddled in a long coat, her hair wind-blown, her face weary and blank. She was drinking from a bottle of plum wine, but she put it away when she saw him walking across the yard.

"How'd you know I was coming back today?" he said as he sat beside her. Miyako gazed at him intently, brushing hair away from her face.

"I didn't know. I just came here to sit. It's something that I do sometimes," she replied in a flat, distant tone, and she looked almost ready to smile when she spoke again. "When did you get back?"

"The train pulled in a little while ago. Didn't you work tonight? Aren't you cold?"

"Yes, of course I worked tonight. I don't feel cold," she said. They sat in silence for several moments, and he had the feeling that something wasn't right, that something had happened to Miyako.

"Well, we may as well go in. Are you all right?"

"I'm fine," she said. They walked inside, and Sky got a sense of comfort from being back in familiar surroundings. Everything looked just as it had before he went to Karatsu. He knew that Miyako had come in now and then to clean the house, but he didn't ask her about it, thinking that it would probably make her uncomfortable.

He turned on the lamp and turned to see her coming into the room, pausing by the door while she kicked off her black high-heels as though giving the action little or no thought. She was dressed all in black-short black skirt, tight black sweater, and black stockings-clothes she had worn to work in the bar. She looked around like she was in an unfamiliar place, and she gave the impression that she was ill at ease. Sky watched her with silent concern, noticing that she looked tired but otherwise unchanged.

"You want some tea?" he asked.

"No."

Miyako turned around abruptly as though remembering something that had been forgotten. She walked across the room to fetch the bottle of wine and her cigarettes from her coat. She sat down at the *kotatsu* as Sky went to the kitchen to fix some tea. When he returned, Miyako was taking a long drink from the bottle. He sat across from her, setting his cup of tea in front of him.

"How did you like Kyushu?" Miyako asked after a lengthy silence.

"It was all right."

"Yes, I think so. I've been there before. It's a pretty good place," she said without feeling. Their conversation continued, but in a sparing and superficial way. She tried to keep her face averted from him, but he could see that her eyes were red and swollen as if from crying.

"Don't you think you've had enough to drink?" Sky asked, and Miyako laughed softly, without humor.

"No. I don't think so. But that's pretty funny, coming from you."

"I guess you're right. Still, my bad habits don't have to be yours," he said, shrugging his shoulders and standing up. He looked down, noticing that the wine bottle was almost empty.

"I'm pretty beat, so I'm going to have to go to sleep now. How about you? Aren't you tired?"

"Yes, I'm tired. Old people get tired easily, you know. I'll be there in a little while."

He shook his head and sat down next to her. He took her hand, but she pulled it away from him. He tried to look into her eyes, but she turned away from him.

"You're not old, not at all. You ought to stop talking about it so much. What you should do now is get some sleep. You look like you could use it. Sitting up by yourself getting drunk isn't a good thing to do. Take it from somebody who knows."

Miyako sat quietly for several moments, but he could

see the beginnings of a smile start along the edges of her mouth and grow until it brightened her whole face. She put her hand in his and spoke. "You're very convincing. Go on ahead, and I'll be there soon."

"That's better," he said, and he left the room.

町 光 青

Sky was lying in the *futon* listening to the sound of the rain when Miyako came into the bedroom. She took off her skirt and sweater and walked over to look out the rain-streaked window.

"Did you think of me while you were in Karatsu?" she asked, her voice soft, nearly inaudible, her eyes still on the rain.

"All the time," he said, and she turned around, smiling like she was doing everything possible to keep from doing so.

"Is that true?"

"It's true."

Miyako came toward him, her thick hair swinging as she moved gracefully through the room that was beginning to fill with rain-filtered daylight. She sat on the *tatami* beside him, looking directly at him, as though searching for meaning in his expression. He was unable to detect any signs of aging in her face. In fact, aside from appearing to be tired and in need of sleep, she had never been more lovely in his eyes.

Having been away from Miyako for some time, certain things about her that had faded from Sky's memory during his stay in Karatsu came back to him in a dizzying rush of consciousness: the intense blackness of her thick, coarse hair, the fact that her flawless skin was so strikingly pale, the expressive quality of her dark eyes, the chrysanthemum tattoo, and the reality of how small she actually was. The room was still dark, but, for a moment it was flooded with a soft but powerful glow, something in her nature about which she would never speak, and of which she wasn't even completely aware.

"Were you crying earlier?" he asked, breaking the silence, and she looked down and away from him.

"Yes."

"Why?"

"It's just that there are times when I don't want to be alone. Do you know?"

"Yes, I know. Being alone is something I know about. It's bad sometimes."

Miyako nodded and stood up. She took off the rest of her clothes and got under the comforter, moving close alongside him. She was shivering slightly as she rested her head at an angle against his shoulder.

"There are times when I don't like to be alone. Times when I feel scared," she said softly, her voice drained of bitterness.

"I understand."

She turned away from him and held her hands in the air, staring at them, as he found himself doing. She wore a number of rings, including one that he had bought for her one day-a plain silver band that she wore on her right hand and never took off. She dropped her hands abruptly, and he moved to hold her close. The sun was coming up over Yokohama, all but invisible in the rain-choked sky where clouds were moving slowly southward.

A Town Where Lights Are Blue

町 光 青

Sky woke up late in the afternoon and saw Miyako across the room, hurriedly getting dressed. She was pulling on her stockings when, in her haste to get home to prepare for work, she fell to the floor in a quick and graceless motion. She landed in a tangle of arms, legs, and flying hair. She shook hair from her eyes, looking dazed, until they both exploded into laughter. She then stood up, no longer laughing, and looked directly at him through torrents of hair.

"What are you looking at?" she asked.

"I'm looking at you, lady. Mostly at your great legs. I don't mean anything by it."

"I think you mean something by it," she said, her voice lowered, husky, seductive.

"All right. I guess I mean something by it," he said, and she laughed heartily and ran over to kneel beside him. She kissed him slowly, breaking away only because she knew she had to.

"I'd at least like to think so!" she then said, standing up and walking away quickly. "I'm sorry. I want to stay, but I can't. It's late, and I have to get ready for work. I've got to hurry now."

Miyako stood before the mirror and straightened her clothes as she put on dark red lipstick. She then ran a brush hurriedly through her hair and frowned, not pleased by the reflection that she saw. She left the room and came back just seconds later, buttoning her coat. She extended her hand so that he could hold it in the few seconds she had left. Sky thought that she looked full of life, very happy. It was a rare and precious moment, and he was glad to be sharing in it.

"Sorry. Can't stay. I'll see you later," she said. "Good-bye."

Miyako ran into the other room and out onto the steps, where she hastily stepped into her shoes before running out into the late afternoon rain.

A Town Where Lights Are Blue

Chapter Twenty-Seven

Sky felt both anxious and nervous as he walked toward the Akabashi on his second day back in Yokohama. The place had always been a kind of touchstone, the true reason for his being in Japan at all. In spite of his night-oriented schedule, he maintained a routine based on work, and the Akabashi was the locus of that. He was excited but uneasy about returning to work, returning to music. He had practiced almost daily while staying at Mrs. Igawa's inn, but he knew that it wasn't the same as working with a group. He wanted to get back to work, but he didn't want to let his sidemen down. After years of playing, he still felt nervous each time he played. He took his time in getting to the club, enjoying the feel of the busy streets, with their flashes of neon and their crowds surging with energy and excitement.

When he arrived at the Akabashi, the place was all but empty. He walked up to the bandstand and stood near the piano. It looked familiar yet somehow alien. He felt uneasy about being in the nearly deserted club, but he had never felt that way in the past. He'd always enjoyed his time alone with the piano and the sad, sensual air of the place after the noise had subsided and the lights had gone down. He looked around, getting a sense of familiarity from the chairs stacked on the tables, the pictures of his heroes, and the relatively clean air as yet untouched by smoke, perfume, sweat, and noise. He sat down at the piano and sat staring at the keyboard. He then looked across the deserted stage. Kenji's drums sat silent and shining in the dim light. He smiled and began playing a few tentative chords.

Sky started out slowly but confidently. He began toying with favorite bits and pieces of Beethoven's Ninth Symphony and then began to ramble with structured abandon through almost every kind of music he'd ever played or just heard. He wove fragments and shards of ragtime, boogie-woogie, baroque, R&B, blues, honky-tonk country, and jazz into his playing. The blend of these elements made for a dissonant, roaring, disquieting, and overwhelmingly joyous montage of pure sound that was real and intensely personal. He played from his heart, from his memory, as he settled deeper into the music and broke free of time.

After a while Sky became aware of another sound in complement to what he was doing. Someone was weaving riffs and runs over, around, and through his own improvisations. He looked over to his left and saw Mikio, sitting on Kenji's drummer's throne, his hands wrapped intently around a harmonica. His long hair was flying and his feet were tapping on the floor, causing it to shake. The music that he was making was peripheral to, and yet totally fused with, Sky's roaring crescendos and shimmering, serpentine vamping and comping. Mikio was actually a pretty good harmonica player. He was adept in the blues idiom and knew all the great players: both Sonnyboy Williamsons, Little Walter, Sonny Terry, Lazy Lester, and many Sky had never heard of. He could play full, rich chords and could bend notes in a way that defied scales but was nonetheless musical. Few people knew that he played, but Sky had heard him before, on all-night drinking binges or at home when everything else was quiet. The music that the two men made started off as two swirling, shouting, undulating voices and eventually became one voice as the music built and held back and surged and receded. Sky finished his playing with a single, deliberately dissonant, note, and Mikio followed suit with a wailing, swaggering, wrenching flourish on the harp, in the style known as cross-harp to some and Lydian mode to others. A heavy silence moved across the stage when they stopped playing. Sky and Mikio looked worn out, near sleep, and then they burst into laughter.

"At least you haven't forgotten how to play the thing. When did you get back, John?"

"Yesterday."

"It's good to have you back," Mikio said. He then got up and walked over to the bar. He returned with two bottles of beer. He gave one to Sky, who was still seated at the piano, and then pulled a chair up onto the stage. He took a pack of cigarettes from his shirt pocket. He got one lit and then offered one to Sky. They sat in the silence of the room, looking exhausted but happy.

"Are you ready to start playing again?" Mikio asked, breaking the silence.

"Yes, I've been ready for a long time. I'd like to start tonight."

"That would suit me. We've missed your presence, that's for sure. It sounds to me like you've been woodshedding a little bit."

"Well, it turns out that I had access to a piano where I was staying down south. I tried to get into something when I could."

"How'd you like it down there?" Mikio asked. Like some

A Town Where Lights Are Blue

people Sky had met in Yokohama, Mikio regarded all of Kyushu, in fact any place away from Yokohama or Tokyo, as the sticks, the boondocks, a place to be avoided at all costs.

"It was all right. I stayed in a nice little place, and I met some good people. It's quieter there, of course. The pace is slower than here."

"I know what you mean. I've been down that way, just passing through. I'm afraid it's a little too slow to suit me," Mikio said, and Sky smiled. Mikio was a big-city boy to the core.

"It was quiet, all right, but I kind of liked it."

"You planning to move any time soon?" Mikio asked, smiling slyly.

"One never knows," Sky said in a melodramatic tone that caused Mikio to laugh.

"Sorry to lose you, but I guess you'll be happier."

"What about Kenji? Yasujiro? They okay?"

"They're getting along all right, about the same as always. I imagine they're still asleep now. I understand they had a rough night."

"Is that right?"

"Yes. I'm afraid their pursuit of the dilettante's life is getting the best of them," Mikio said, mock-seriously, and they laughed again.

"It's good to know that some things never change. Well, I'm going back home, get some food and change clothes. Mikio, are you sure you want me to come back tonight?" Sky said. He glanced at his watch. It was nearly three o'clock, which was later than he thought.

"Yes, I'm sure. I'll tell the others. They'll be glad to hear that you're back."

"That's good to know. Hey, how about Tsushima? How's he doing?"

"How can you ever tell?"

"Yes, he does make it difficult. I'd better get out of here and start getting myself together for tonight. You sure you don't want me to loosen up for a few more days or something?"

"I heard the way you were playing. Remember? You sound ready to me."

They got their coats and left. The cleaning women who had been there had long since left. Mikio locked up and they walked down the alley and out onto the street.

"I'll see you later," Sky said as they parted ways.

"See you later, John."

Sky and Mikio walked away in different directions down the crowded street. Sky no longer felt nervous. He was in a hurry to get ready and come back to the club, back to music. It was where he belonged. He had never felt more certain about anything.

町 光 青

Sky's first night back with the quartet turned out better than he had hoped. His relative lack of practice and his nervousness were evident at first. He blew a few introductions and missed a note here and there, but he quickly settled in and then began to sail through the sets of pop tunes and jazz standards. He would occasionally do something unexpected, like lay in some stride choruses. His sidemen, rather than be put off by such touches, more often than not responded with offbeat flourishes of their own.

A Town Where Lights Are Blue

The quartet was relaxed yet tight. Mikio's guitar work was alternately spare and explosive as he ripped into choruses with blistering speed or hung back, making what he wasn't doing as interesting as what he was. Yasujiro's bass lines were sinuous and insistent, easing into loping lines or ostinato patterns that lay at the precise bottom of the music. Kenji's drumming fused in perfectly with the efforts of the others, with syncopated bass accents, crackling rim shots, subtle work on the cymbals, including the high-hat, and jagged, staccato snare rolls. When the time came to take their first break, they had been either perfectly roaring or crystalline on every song. Each member of the quartet was infused with a new-found energy, and they went into a furiously up-tempo rundown of "I'll Be Seeing You" as their break song. When they got through it, everyone in the room was on their feet, cheering and applauding, and the quartet left the stage, smiling, exhausted, and elated. Sky was sweating and weary, but anxious to get back to the music. It could be like that when things were going well. He walked over to a nearby table and joined his sidemen, and they leaned back in their chairs, smoking, drinking, and laughing.

"Sky, where'd you pick up those West Coast bop riffs?" Kenji asked.

"Don't really know. Must have heard them on some record or something."

"I think we ought to run through "C Jam Blues" next set," Yasujiro said enthusiastically, and they all agreed to give the old Duke Ellington classic a try. They'd used it often in the past but hadn't played it in a while.

町 光 青

The remaining sets seemed to pass by very quickly, and it was almost closing time before Sky had any real idea of the time. He thought back to a veteran tenor saxophone player he had met while on the road in Nebraska in his earliest years of playing. The man was in his fifties, and had never become famous, but he played with all the fire and drive of someone half his age. Sky had especially liked his work on "Sentimental Journey" because he gave the old tune a whole new slant and energy and heart to burn. Sky talked with him between sets, and the aging sax player, his hair soaked and hanging in his eyes, his tie loose, his dark baggy suit streaked and stained, had told Sky that musicians told time by their own clock, and that made them always a little bit behind the beat of straight-life time. He hadn't thought much about it at the time, but, as he continued playing music over the years, he began to see the sense and truth in the veteran hornman's take on time and music.

町 光 青

The band was playing a slow dance tune when they became aware of the lateness of the hour, and Sky went abruptly into the opening chords of "Speak Low." They broke into the melody in double-time tempo, and Sky took the first solo, borrowing from Monk, his aunt, Blind John Davis, and himself, the notes roaring out filled with all the good and bad things that he knew, and Mikio took over from him seamlessly, tearing into an upper-register solo that was staggering in its power and brevity. Kenji then traded four bar breaks with Sky, and the song ended in a controlled frenzy

A Town Where Lights Are Blue

of pounding piano chords, thumping bass lines, cymbal splashes, and surging guitar riffs that somehow all dovetailed into a perfect finish. The Akabashi's patrons were clapping and shouting for more. They were keyed up and lively, and many of them came up to the edge of the stage to tell the musicians how much they had enjoyed the music that night. Sky and the others thanked them, enjoying the compliments, but holding back on any promises of encores. They'd quit when they should have. Anything else would have been a letdown after what had come before. The bartenders and waitresses began their preparations for closing so that they could go out and enjoy themselves. The members of the quartet sat at a table in the back, too tired even for their ritual card game. They sipped their drinks, feeling drained yet capable of a second wind.

"Well, we've got a party to go to. Are you about ready?" Kenji said, turning to Yasujiro.

"I'm ready," he replied. They got up and began putting on their overcoats, pausing by the door as they waved goodbye.

"Ready to go?" Mikio said to Sky. They had enjoyed the sudden silence at first, but it began to get on their nerves as they sat in the quiet club.

"Sure. Let's make it."

They got into their coats just as Tsushima was turning off the last of the house lights. They walked down the alley and up to the street beyond. Taxis rushed by and the street was still crowded and lively, despite the lateness of the hour. They walked along, restless but at a loss as to where to go.

"Where do you feel like going?" Mikio asked.

"I don't know. Any place you decide on is all right with me."

"I know a place not far from here you might like," Mikio said. Sky nodded in reply, and they walked a few blocks until they came to a brightly lit bar. It was a place that Sky had neither been to or heard of.

"What do you think?" Mikio said as they paused on the street outside the bar.

"Looks fine to me. Let's go on in and grab a table."

After they had sat through a few rounds, Mikio told Sky that he felt like dancing and he walked over to a nearby table where a couple of young women were sitting. He danced through a few songs with the older-looking of the two women. She was a tall, dark girl with long, carefully styled hair. She was dressed in black and heavily made-up. When Mikio returned to the table, both women accompanied him. He introduced the girl he'd been dancing with as Asami. The other girl's name was Michiyo. She wasn't as tall as Asami, and she seemed less outgoing. She wore a red dress, in contrast to Asami's dark clothes.

The two women sat at the table and talked with each other as Mikio and Sky exchanged glances and shrugs across the table. After a while, Mikio and Asami got up to dance again, leaving Sky alone with Michiyo, who seemed cool and remote.

"Do you want another drink?" Sky asked, wanting to break the ice but feeling awkward. Michiyo looked at him and said nothing, but her expression conveyed a clear sense of annoyance and boredom. She turned away without answering and looked out onto the dance floor.

"Where do you work?" Sky asked when the waitress brought him another beer. Michiyo only glared at him. Sky broke off his attempts at communication and turned his attention to the song that was playing-Otis Redding's version of "Cigarettes And Coffee."

町 光 青

They stayed in the bar for what seemed to Sky like a very long time. The elation that he had felt after leaving the Akabashi had waned and was turning into something more like fatigue. Mikio, however, was having a good time, so Sky settled in, sharing an occasional unpleasant silence with Michiyo, drinking steadily, and listening to the jukebox. By the time that Mikio returned to the table with Asami for the last time, Sky was very tired and more than a little drunk.

"Let's go," Mikio said cheerfully.

"I'm all for that," Sky replied.

"We're going over to Asami's house," Mikio said once they got outside.

"All right," Sky replied without enthusiasm, unsure how he would fit into the current set-up. Asami and Michiyo were walking ahead of them, talking in low tones, when they stopped abruptly and turned around.

"There's no need for you to come along," Michiyo said, the first words Sky had heard her speak. It was clear that her remark was intended only for him. Mikio turned to him, grinning and shrugging his shoulders.

"I'll see you later on," he said, walking away.

"Sure. I'll see you at the club tomorrow."

Sky was left standing alone at the mouth of a narrow alley. Looking down it, he could see a blue neon sign blinking through the fog. It advertised a bar that was still open, and without hesitation he began walking toward it.

町 光 青

Sky stayed in the bar until past seven that morning. The place was small and gave the impression of being crowded, even though he was practically the only person there besides the owner and his wife. The place was dark and there was a jukebox at the rear of the room that poured out a steady stream of Japanese pop music from the current day and well into the past.

Sky talked for a long time with the owner/bartender. His wife, a pleasant middle-aged woman, tended to work the lower portion of the bar, chatting with the few customers who came in and out. Sky was considering calling for another round when he decided that it was time to go home. He settled his tab and shook hands with the owner, who told him to come back soon. He left the bar and walked up to the street. He hailed a cab and nearly fell asleep as it took him towards home. The sun had been up for some time, but the streets were still nearly empty. He paid the driver and walked down the road along the canal. He was crossing the yard toward his house, which had never looked so inviting, when he realized that it was his birthday. He was twenty-eight years old.

A Town Where Lights Are Blue

Chapter Twenty-Eight

Sky didn't see or hear from Sayoko for some time after he returned from Karatsu. He dropped by her house a few times and tried to call her, but he was never able to get in touch with her. He'd been back in Yokohama for quite a while when he finally saw her come into the Akabashi in the company of a heavy-set American man who was dressed in an expensive dark suit. Sky left the stage at the end of the first set and Sayoko stopped by to ask him to join her and her new friend. He didn't feel comfortable about it, but he walked over to join them.

The man with Sayoko was apparently rich, but he was also loud and ill-mannered. He told Sky his name, but he talked so much and so fast that he was never able to remember it from that time on. He mostly listened, and Sayoko hardly spoke at all. She seemed unusually restrained and aloof. Sky guessed her friend to be around fifty. His hair was dark, glossy, and carefully styled and it looked like it had been colored with something outside nature. He was very drunk, slurping scotch and soda while Sayoko kept pace with him, drinking gin and tonic. She was obviously drunk, but subdued, like a storm ready to explode with fury, and apparently all but oblivious of Sky's presence at the table. There was something unknown and lethal just beneath the surface of Sayoko's bland, careless manner that gave him a cold sweat, but he had no idea of what this thing might be, or if it even existed.

"I've been over to this part of the world lots of times, and I've got a real fondness for ladies like this one," the man said in a voice that was much louder than necessary. He was pointing at Sayoko, his large, bejeweled hand sweating and shaking with something that seemed massively unhealthy. Sky nodded, but he had no idea how to respond to such a statement.

"I see," he said, glancing at his watch. He had some time left on his break, but he was in a hurry to leave.

"Oh, yes. This little number here showed me a time last night I won't soon forget," the man said, almost shouting. He then collapsed into laughter, sloshing his drink onto the lapel of his expensive suit. Sky began to feel a light-headed sensation of slowly emerging sickness that grew from some small dark place within himself and spread to every atom of his being.

Sayoko's "new friend" was loud, sloppy, and almost insanely insensitive, and Sky felt intensely uncomfortable around him, listening to his references to Sayoko, and Japanese people in general, rendered in a high-pitched whine. His language was crude and liberally laced with derogatory slurs, and Sky had a flash go through him that the only way to stop him was to hit him, hard and often, knock him to the floor and beat him with his fists and his cane and his beer bottle until he was wet with sweat and blood and beer, but he just looked blank and did nothing until he knew that he had to leave or he'd do something he'd never be able to undo. Sayoko returned to the table, having gone away for a few minutes. Her usually graceful movements were marred by her drunken state and the glow in her eyes was piteously dulled. The man stopped talking, though only for a moment, and lurched across the table, urging Sayoko to sit near him. She sat down, almost meekly, looking totally lost.

"She tells me you're old friends, practically brother and sister," the man said, sending a shock down Sky's spine. It was a peculiar thing to say, made all the more strange by the hint of truth it seemed to contain.

"We're friends," Sky said, his voice flat and without feeling, his head down.

"I'm her friend, too, but maybe I'm a better friend to her than you could ever be," the man said, and Sky's blank expression changed. The loathing that he felt for the man could no longer be contained, and it came to the surface, causing Sayoko to look away and shudder, although the man didn't appear to notice. Sky looked around, his head spinning and his mouth dry, and he saw Mikio waving to him from the stage. Kenji was already behind his trap set. The next set was almost ready to begin, and Sky got up, still feeling lightheaded and sick.

"I've got to get back to work. It was good to see you again, Sayoko," he said, and she replied in a slurred, breathy tone that sent chills racking through him.

"Good-bye, old friend."

Sky returned to the bandstand and saw that the others were already tuning up and adjusting their gear. He got a bottle of beer from a passing waitress and sat down at the piano, feeling more than tired, feeling used up and finished, ancient. He broke into a rapid-fire version of "Cherokee" that almost, if not quite, caught his sidemen off guard. They caught on quickly and then joined in, never missing a beat. The song was short, furious, and very fast, but it ended abruptly. Sky then led the quartet into an extended version of "Angel Eyes" that was alive with rippling pain and raw beauty. Sayoko and her companion left shortly after the song ended. The rest of the night passed uneventfully for Sky, except for his receiving a call from Hanako, Ota's sister. She told him that Ota was being released from the hospital, and that he'd be home within a couple of days. He thanked her for the news and told her he'd come by to visit as soon as he could.

Chapter Twenty-Nine

When Sky went to visit Ota, the weather was clear, bright, and almost warm. It looked for a time like March might turn out to be a month of fair weather, but Sky noticed that the late winter sun still held a chill that couldn't be denied.

Sky was met at the door by Hanako, who greeted him warmly and led him into the living room. Ota was lying on the sofa watching an old American detective show on television while Hiroshi talked animatedly on the phone. He nodded in Sky's direction but didn't detach himself from his conversation. Sky walked over and shook hands with Ota.

"You're looking pretty good, old friend," Sky said, smiling. Ota looked better than he had in the hospital, but it would have been difficult to look any worse than he had at that time. In spite of this, Sky was still taken aback by Ota's pale and weakened appearance.

"I'm starting to come around. I feel a little better, day by day," Ota said, and Sky was encouraged by the strength and clarity of his tone.

"I'm sorry I never made it back to the hospital for another visit. I felt bad about that."

Ota nodded and looked serious. "You had things to do."

"That's true. Tell me, did Omura Sayoko ever come by to see you? I asked her to do that for me."

"So I have you to thank for that. Yes, she came by. A couple of times, in fact. I wasn't at my best during those visits, but to tell you the truth, seeing her always made me feel better. How was your exile in Kyushu?"

"It was all right," Sky replied. There was a pause, and for a few moments he had to struggle to find something to say, even something safe and simple. "How are you feeling now, really?" he asked at length.

"I thought I'd be up and around by now. It's coming slower than I expected. I just feel weak and tired most of the time, and I'm not comfortable with that," Ota said, taking his time as though trying hard to express himself clearly. Sky realized that weakness and fatigue had to be alien states of being for Ota. He had never met anyone with more love of life and personal energy. Lying around day after day had to be very difficult for him.

"Well, take it light, and you'll be running circles around everybody else just like always, and real soon, too," Sky said, and Ota smiled, some of the old energy that Sky recalled from earlier times flooding back into his face and eyes.

"Not soon enough to suit me. Did you happen to bring any beer with you?"

Sky laughed, feeling relieved. For the first time during the visit, he relaxed. "Believe it or not I didn't, but I could slip out and get us some."

"No, don't bother," Ota said. He then called to Hanako, who came into the room from the kitchen. Hanako was a slender, quiet young woman. She looked younger than her years, but her characteristically serious expression usually offset any sense of youth. She exchanged some heated words with Ota. She then reluctantly agreed to go to the local shop for some beer. As Hanako was opening the door, Hiroshi ended his phone conversation, muttered his good-byes, and left the house with her.

町 光 青

Sky and Ota talked into the late afternoon as they drank the beer that Hanako had brought back from the shop. They talked of happy times, plans for the future, and made no further mention of Ota's injuries, or of the circumstances that had brought them about. Hanako fixed a simple but delicious meal of rice and fish and even joined them for a time, enjoying being a part of the good-natured talk. Sky and Ota praised her cooking and she gave the impression of being self-conscious but very pleased by the attention and compliments. She cleared the table and left them, returning to the kitchen to clean up.

"Do you have to work tomorrow?" Ota asked.

"Sure. You know, the same old routine. But, you know, this has been a great day. I've really missed talking to you."

"It has been a good day. I'm glad you were able to come by. You know, there were times when I was in the hospital up in Tokyo, and you were down in Karatsu, when I felt like I wouldn't see you any more," Ota said seriously, and Sky looked up, surprised.

"You really felt that way?"

"Just now and then. But, you did come back, and I'm glad. By the way, Miyumi came by for a little while yesterday, and we had a nice visit. Tell me, what ever happened with you and Omura Sayoko?"

"I'm not real sure," Sky said, trying, but failing, to come up with a suitable reply.

A Town Where Lights Are Blue

"I see."

It wasn't very late, but Sky felt tired, and he knew that he had to leave. "It's time for me to go," he said, standing up.

"Hanako, just one more beer?" Ota said.

"No!" she responded emphatically from the kitchen, and both Sky and Ota laughed.

"You can't argue with that," Sky said, and Ota grinned and shook his head.

"Not successfully, anyway."

"You take care of yourself, and let me know if you need anything."

"I'll be in touch," Ota said, and Sky waved and let himself out, pausing by the kitchen to say good night to Hanako.

町 光 青

Sky arrived at his house feeling tired but in no way sleepy. He fixed a small glass of cognac and another of ice water and picked out a Lennie Tristano record, trying to absorb his complex ideas and focused energy. These were, in his mind, wonderful things to behold, but invariably difficult if not impossible to work into his own music. There were some musicians he listened to with no real sense of learning riffs or chord changes. It was a spiritual thing-all sadness, all joy, all real. Night had fallen on Yokohama in a definitive way, but the warm light inside the small room and the alternately rippling and cascading notes from a piano style much different from his own filled his house and his heart with a pleasantly melancholy unfamiliar feeling that might have been something like peace.

Chapter Thirty

Sky didn't see Sayoko often after his return to Yokohama. He hadn't seen her in the Akabashi in quite some time when he ran into her in an all-night bar. She was in the company of Sumiko when they joined him at his table at a little after three in the morning. They exchanged perfunctory greetings and then sat down to order drinks.

"Where's your new friend?" Sky asked, noticing that Sayoko looked more achingly beautiful than ever, but also tired and somehow beaten.

"Him? He's nobody," she replied, and Sky shook his head and smiled ruefully.

"I think the world of you, Sayoko, but you've got one annoying habit. You keep referring to people who seem to matter to you as 'nobody'. Are you still seeing him?"

"Of course. As a matter of fact, I'm seeing him tomorrow. You take things too seriously, Sky. You don't have to worry about him," she said, and he was encouraged by something that he saw briefly light up her eyes. It was a spark of humor, or spirit, some important part of her being that had been missing when he first saw her that night.

"I'm not worried about him. Why should I be? I'm worried about you," he said, and she relaxed. She looked pleased, if surprised, and she smiled warmly as she put her hand on his arm.

A Town Where Lights Are Blue

町 光 青

They stayed in the bar for hours, drinking steadily and speaking little, searching for words while listening to music, though Sky could only recall a few titles: "Strange," "Jim," "Don't Even Kick it Around," and "Breeze From the East." It was past six when he turned to Sayoko.

"I'm getting out of here. You coming along?"

Sayoko looked at him like she'd never seen him before, and her words in response seemed uncharacteristically harsh. "You know I can't do that. I've got to keep Sumiko company."

"All right. I'll see you ladies later on," he said and then left the bar.

町 光 青

Sky didn't see Sayoko again until she dropped by his house on an overcast day in the middle of the week. The sky was dark and forbidding, but her mood was bright, buoyant and full of life, at least at first.

"It's good to see you again," Sky said, and she walked over to sit across the kotatsu from him. She was dressed in a black jersey dress, her hair was newly styled, and her skin gave off a dark glow. Words like "beauty" seemed to Sky wildly insufficient in trying to convey Sayoko's physical presence at moments like this. Her spirit was radiant, and her outer self only complemented it. Her loveliness was occasionally devastating, almost painful, too much for anyone to truly comprehend.

"It's good to see you, too," she said, her tone warm and unaffected.

"I don't see much of you these days."

"I know, and I'm sorry for that. I've been busy lately. I've been well, and I hope you've been the same. I wanted to make sure that you got the news."

"News?" Sky realized then that her tone was too bright, like sunshine that stings the eyes, or like music that's perfect but a little too loud. His hands shook as he lit a cigarette.

"I'm getting married soon. I'm making sure that all my friends know."

For a moment Sky thought it was a joke. He almost laughed, but choked it back as he became aware that something for which he was unprepared was about to become known. "When is this taking place?" he said, still thinking that there was a chance she might be joking.

"I can't say for sure, but soon. Very soon. He just proposed a few days ago. I knew that he was going to do it, I just didn't know when," she said, and Sky knew then that she was serious. He noticed a large diamond ring, an engagement ring, on her left hand. It was garish and cheap-looking in appearance, but he thought that it was probably expensive. It looked rotten and ugly against the beauty and delicacy of her hand.

"Who is it?" he asked, knowing, but not wanting to hear, the answer.

"My new lover. You know. You met him at the Akabashi. He wants to get married, the sooner the better. He wants to take me away, Sky. He wants to take me to America," she said, as though she were speaking of going to some distant galaxy, beyond the realm of technology and possibility. Her voice was childlike, wistful, almost cheerful, and it gave him a chill that traveled up his back in a way that was like the slow and lethal movements of snakes he had seen long ago, in Vietnam, what now seemed like a hundred years ago. He found the news impossible to accept, preposterous, while simultaneously recognizing it as the truth. These things happened, making reality far more bizarre than the most calculated fantasy.

"Sayoko, this is a little hard for me to take in. It's none of my business, but don't you at least want to think about it for a while? You're young. You don't need this yet. I'd like to see something right happen to you, but I don't think this is it."

"I'm getting married because I'm in love, Sky. Is that so difficult to understand?" she asked, her usual husky tone becoming momentarily shrill.

"I guess it shouldn't be, but in this case it is. At least for me it is. Marriage can seem like an easy thing to get into, but getting out of it is much harder. You really ought to think about this some."

"What you say makes sense, but I've thought about it as much as I care to. This is my decision. It's what I want to do. He wants to take me away. I want to do that, Sky. I want to leave Japan," she said, her voice hollow and flat.

"But, you love Japan, Sayoko. I may not understand much about you, but I know that much. It couldn't be more plain. This is your home," he said, this last sentence the hardest to say, because he envied her on this point. He wasn't sure that he had something as simple as a place to call home. Japan, what it meant, whatever that was, was a matter-of-fact but crucial anchor for Sayoko, and Sky got the disturbing feeling that she was pulling slowly and painfully away from the mooring that such an anchor provided.

"I don't know about all that. I only know I want to go away. I don't belong here, Sky. You could never understand, not really. You think you know about me, but you don't. I won't belong somewhere else, either, but I can take a chance," Sayoko said, her voice resigned, having aged eons in a few seconds. The worst part of it all for Sky was that a fair amount of what she had said had the ring of truth.

"Well, you sound like your mind's made up. I don't know much, but I know you can't change people. I don't like what you're doing here, not at all, but I guess I have to accept it, and wish you well, for whatever that's worth," he said, and Sayoko smiled, coming back into a semblance of something that was familiar to him. He felt sick, exhausted, and dizzy. It was as though he had fought ten men. Having done that couldn't have hurt him more or made him more profoundly tired.

町 光 青

Sayoko stayed on at Sky's house a little longer after passing on her devastating news, seeming at once anxious beyond words to leave and unwilling to go. She was talkative in a way that he'd never noticed before, and, although he was glad for her presence in his life, no matter what the circumstances, the seconds and minutes seemed to drag by, and he was grateful when the time came for her to leave.

"I'll talk to you soon, Sky. You can come to the wedding, of course, if you'd like to. It would make me feel good if you did," she said, and he nodded, standing up slowly and stiffly. She reached awkwardly across the kotatsu and handed him his cane. They looked openly at each other, and he was gratified to see that the wild, fevered look that had been animating her eyes throughout much of her visit had vanished. It had been replaced by a calm, hopeful gaze that seemed to look toward a chance of forgiveness and understanding. It made Sky relax, but he realized that, his years in Yokohama to the contrary, he knew nothing about Japan, nothing about life in general. He felt like nothing more than a pair of weary eyes, exhausted from watching life drift inexorably by him, sometimes slow and tranquil, and sometimes rapid and savage.

"We'll see," he said, at last looking away from her. He was filled with loathing and anger, yet his voice reached Sayoko in a gentle tone, and she looked relieved. Her eyes narrowed and words finally failed her. She fought hard for something to say.

"Take care of yourself," she said, the honesty of her tone frightening and clean, like a white-hot knife blade cauterizing an open wound. He then knew that they shared something, even if they were both incapable of articulating what it was. For Sky, it didn't matter. It was enough that it existed at all.

"You, too, Sayoko. Good-bye," he said, and she left the house quietly, like a master thief departing the scene of a meticulously planned and flawlessly executed crime.

Chapter Thirty-One

March in Yokohama began as a series of days of rain that later gave way to snow. In these days of bitter weather, Sky concentrated on his music, often putting in hours of practice on his own in addition to the time spent in rehearsals with the group. He heard from Sayoko only once after the day when she dropped by his house with her startling news. She called to let him know the time and place of her wedding. He congratulated her and told her that he would attend if he could. He was unable to stop thinking about her wedding plans for days after she had told him about them, but in time he learned to accept the situation. Like many things in life, it was beyond his control.

He stopped by to visit Ota from time to time to check on his progress. Overall, his convalescence seemed to be going slowly, but well. He was stoic about his predicament, but he occasionally complained about not being able to get out. Sky could sense subtle changes in Ota's character. He was quieter, less self-assured, and Sky wasn't sure if these changes were for the better or worse. Miyumi was often with Ota, possessive and protective in an understated way.

But in general, Sky was absorbed by his music. He wrote new songs, arranged old standards that the quartet often played, and thought about expanding the group, maybe adding a trumpet or saxophone, although he never mentioned this idea to the others in the group. In some ways the notion of a bigger group was interesting and exciting, while in other ways it seemed self-defeating. He thought that the addition of other instruments might ultimately hurt the sense of cohesion within the quartet. He kept busy through a bitter cold snap as March wore on, and the brief warm period that had marked the earliest days of his return from the south faded completely from his memory.

Chapter Thirty-Two

Miyako came by the Akabashi one Friday night not long before closing time. It was the first time in weeks that Sky had seen her. She came in and waved to him, then sat down at a table near the stage, where she remained until the last set ended. Sky's sidemen had other plans and didn't go through their usual ritual of playing cards. They mumbled good-byes and left the club in a rush.

Sky got up slowly and walked over to sit on the edge of the stage, and Miyako came over to join him. Her hair was up in an elaborate style that seemed to Sky somewhat uncharacteristic of her, and she was wearing a long black evening dress. Her overall appearance suggested that she had just returned from a formal occasion of some kind, and she wore a serene and distant expression that he had never noticed before. She turned to face him, smiling and languid.

"It's been a long time, Miyako," he said, and her expression altered slightly, a subtle shift of meaning in her eyes.

"Yes, it's been a while. I've been very busy," she said, and he nodded in reply as she began to speak again.

"I've missed you," she said, and there was in her voice a sad, soft edge that occasionally eased into it, clearing it of bitterness and always catching him off guard.

"You have?"

"Oh, yes. Haven't you also missed me?"

"Of course."

They sat and talked as the bartenders and waitresses hurried through the routine of cleaning up for closing, until Sky stood up and stretched. He walked over to get his coat, while Miyako walked over to the table to fetch hers.

"Raining out?" he asked.

"No."

"You want to go somewhere?"

"It's up to you, but I'm actually pretty tired."

"Me, too. I hadn't planned on going anywhere except home."

"That sounds good to me," she said, her voice distant and euphoric.

町 光 青

When they arrived at his house Miyako changed into a robe and took down her hair. She then insisted on fixing some food. Working with some rice and vegetables, she paused suddenly to pour some whisky into a glass with ice. She drank it quickly, then poured herself another, while Sky set out a glass of cognac. She then fixed him a glass of ice water.

"You remembered," he said, smiling, and Miyako returned to her cooking with a serious expression.

"I remember everything," she said, and he leaned against the sink, sipping cognac and nodding.

"Me, too."

"Everything?"

"All of it. A hundred percent. Every moment, every expression, every word," he replied, and she looked over at him, pausing in her work, smiling. She wiped her hand across her forehead, looking tired but happy.

Miyako put down the knife she had been using and looked at him in an open way. She paused for several moments and then started working again. "I have something to tell you."

Sky looked away for a moment, reaching for his glass of ice water. "What's that?"

"I'm going to have a baby," she said, and he set the glass down hard, spilling water onto the floor. He then took a long drink and set the glass down carefully, as though it contained nitroglycerin instead of ice water.

"How do you know? Are you sure?" he asked.

Miyako frowned, then laughed quietly, keeping her concentration on her work. "I went to the doctor a few days ago. There's no doubt," she said, and Sky nodded and took a long drink of cognac, then poured some more, nearly filling the glass.

"Do you want to keep the baby?" he asked, not knowing what to expect. They were close, in their way, but there were depths to her that he hadn't begun to fathom. His mind was troubled by cold, hard questions, until he heard the sound of her laughter-natural and spontaneous, like that of someone who's finally able to relax after years of hardship and struggle. It was a brief and subtle moment, but for Sky nothing would ever be the same again.

"That's a silly question. Of course I want to keep the baby. It's my child, Sky," she said, setting her work aside for a moment as she took a drink of whisky. "Yours, too, you know."

"How do you know that?" he asked, his voice thick, and he regretted the question the moment it left his mouth. Miyako gave him a stern look and shook her head. She then smiled, but reluctantly, as if she were dealing with someone incapable of ever learning anything.

"How do I know? How do you think I know? You think that because I'm what I am I can't have the same feelings that other women have? Or know the same things they do? It's just the kind of thing women know, Sky. All women, wherever they live and whatever they do. It's the way things are. You surely must know that."

Sky leaned back, at odds with what to do with his hands. He reached for his cigarettes with one hand and his drink with the other, but then gave up on trying to get either. He had some thinking to do. Miyako continued working, humming softly, going about her chores in a sure way that suggested total concentration. Sky then looked across the room at her and she met his gaze, her expression hard to read.

"That's great. Of course it's great. I'm a little slow on the uptake here, but this is big. This changes everything."

"How?" Miyako asked, and he shook his head.

"In every way. You know that. I just don't know how to talk about something like this. It's something I never expected. But I want it. More than anything else," he said, and Miyako smiled and nodded, continuing her work.

"I mean, except maybe how much I want you. Or, I guess I just don't have the words. It's going to be a girl, of course, and she'll look exactly like you," he said, and Miyako paused and shook her hair back. She was sweating, and looked tired, but she illuminated the poorly lit kitchen in a fundamental yet esoteric way. She walked over and stood in front of him.

"Except with your eyes," she said softly, running her

finger down his cheek.
"How far along are you?"
"Not too far yet."
"How are you? I mean, how do you feel?"
"I feel fine. How should I feel?"
"Fine, I guess. I hope. I just want you to feel as good about this as I do."
"I do."

They didn't talk much during the rest of the evening, not feeling the need for words now that all the important ones had been spoken. Miyako fixed a huge, delicious meal, using only the simplest, most basic ingredients, and they lingered over it, giving up their liquor for pots of hot green tea. They resumed talking after the meal, but only sparingly, drifting now and then into silence while listening to *koto* music and Art Tatum playing solo. They stayed up long enough to see the dim glow of the kitchen light being eclipsed by delicately shifting shades of morning sunlight, and then they left the kitchen.

A Town Where Lights Are Blue

Chapter Thirty-Three

Sky began to give considerable thought to the new direction his life had taken in only a few weeks. It occurred to him that much of his life had been aimless and unfocused. That appeared to be changing, however, and things began to move for him with a sense of energy and urgency that had been missing before. His mind was filled with many things, foremost among them Miyako's news about the baby. He kept this piece of information to himself, just as she did. In truth it took some time for the full import of this piece of news to fully take shape for him, and there were times when, although he knew the contrary to be true, it didn't seem real.

Miyako had begun to spend more time with him at his house. She hadn't given up working, nor even broached the subject of doing so. She had never revealed to him the name of the bar, or bars, where she worked. Sky figured that she had her reasons for this, and in truth he wasn't sure that he really wanted to know.

The prospect of having a child had given Miyako a new perspective on life, and Sky noticed that much of the bitterness that was deeply ingrained in her ebbed away a little each day. It would nonetheless occasionally still surface, taking shape in periods of depression or dark, melancholy silences that nothing could shatter. Sky let this take its course, because he knew there was nothing he could do to change it. It was part of her way, something that he knew would always be a part of her.

Sky took Miyako on a brief trip to Atami, and it was there, on an overcast afternoon, that she told him that she loved him. His first reaction to this new development was one of confusion, almost shock. It was confusing to him for the fundamental reason that he had never truly considered the possibility of such a kind of love coming into his life. Miyako's confession of love opened up doors, horizons, in his life that had seemed closed or distant at best. He then realized that he loved her, and had for some time. It took him a few false starts and some garbled words, but he told her so, there on that cold, windy day on a hillside outside Atami.

Their stay in Atami became an occasion for the breaking down of barriers between Sky and Miyako that had made real communication impossible. These were barriers of bitterness, mistrust, and distance. From that time on, Miyako was subtly changed. On the surface everything was as it had been, but Sky was aware of a transformation. She became less cynical, more direct. From this point on they never exchanged any of the caustic jokes about being "foreigners" that had been a component of many of their conversations from their earliest days together.

It wasn't long after they returned to Yokohama from Atami that they wound up in a fierce argument, as vehement as any they'd ever had. When it was over, and Miyako had left, Sky knew that he'd been wrong to argue with her about the subject of leaving her job. She was going to do this when the time was right, and he knew it, had no doubt about it at all. It had simply been a matter of a clash of two different points of view on a sensitive subject. He regretted the fight, and wasted no time in going to her and telling her so. He realized that his pressing the issue had only increased the intense pressure she was experiencing.

For much of their time together, Sky and Miyako spoke little to each other, and sometimes not at all. The reasons for this were different from those that had brought on silences during the earlier days of their relationship. Before, there had always been a kind of mutual hostility and lack of trust based on fears of rejection that had made communication difficult at best. They now spoke little because they were coming to know one another. Miyako knew something about Sky that was really evident but hard to truly understand-the fact that he was a quiet man who preferred actions to words. As for Sky, he began to see that the drunken arguments, bar room dialogues, street corner assignations, and pain and chaos of her past notwithstanding, Miyako was a very quiet lady.

A Town Where Lights Are Blue

Chapter Thirty-Four

The days of March continued to be bitter and cold and there were many days of nights of rain, although the final traces of snow were now gone. Sky concentrated on work and on thoughts of Miyako and the baby who was to be born in autumn.

Miyako began to spend as much time as she could with Sky, but he realized that she would also need some time away from him as she worked her way through disengaging herself from her old way of life. Sky allowed the changes to take their natural course.

During this period of change, Sky got into the habit of traveling with Yasujiro and Mikio to small towns up and down the coast as a new sense of restlessness came over him. He'd spend nights in bleak hotel rooms, drinking into the night and working on writing new songs and coming up with fresh arrangements of old ones. Yokohama had always instilled in him a sense of something like home, and this feeling remained, but he now frequently felt the need to get away.

Sky and his partners from the band invariably stayed in ancient, inexpensive hotels and inns, usually near the sea. They would settle in for long nights of poker and drinking, Sky sticking mostly to beer during these sessions, although occasionally having a taste for cognac. While staying in a small fishing village some distance south of Yokohama, they spent an aimless evening of drinking, devoid even of shop-talk or cards. They crowded into Mikio's cramped room, drinking in a quick and mechanical way and engaging in sporadic conversation while listening to a radio station that specialized in ballads.

Yasujiro was seated at a small table near the window, wearing a *kimono* spotted with tea stains and soy sauce. He sat slumped forward at the table, smoking and drinking sake from a delicate black lacquer cup that looked like an antique, making it seem out of place in the crowded, cluttered, stuffy room, with its drab brown walls festooned with cheap hanging scrolls. He was sitting across from a stunning young local woman whose name Sky had heard but long since forgotten. She was beautiful but indistinguishable from many others he had seen over the past few weeks. He remembered faces clearly, but not names. This young woman had meticulously styled hair and was dressed in a dark blue *kimono*. She was quiet yet expressive, and Sky was struck by her serene expression that bespoke many interesting secrets just below her calm exterior. Her serenity and grace were at odds with Yasujiro's tired, jaded stare and his look of emptiness and longing for something that lay just beyond his reach. He was talking incessantly, although Sky, who was sitting on the edge of the bed holding a half-forgotten bottle of warm beer, had ceased to hear him, his concentration being fixed on the interchangeable, sentimental, yet oddly affecting ballads emanating nonstop from the radio. He looked up abruptly as though coming out of sleep, set his beer bottle down on the floor, and stood up to leave, pausing as a wave of dizziness assaulted him and then abated.

"I'm going to take a walk," he said, his voice thick and

weary. Mikio had fallen asleep in the chair across the room from him, and Yasujiro and the young woman glanced up and waved as he left.

    Sky walked away from the hotel toward the sea, alone in the early morning calm of the village's main street. The town, although lively and busy during the day, was quiet now, and in fact it had the atmosphere of some deserted place, a ghost town passed by and fallen into neglect in an increasingly technological world. It seemed sad to Sky, even as he acknowledged that his appraisal of the situation was inaccurate. He walked on until he approached the shoreline, and there he paused, resting on his cane for a few moments in a cool, predawn breeze flavored by the sea stretching endlessly in front of him and the pines through which he had just walked.

    Sky saw some jagged rocks stretching far out into the open sea, and he made his way awkwardly among them, the water rough and heavy all around him. He came to what appeared to be the end point and then stopped, savoring the cool wind that cleansed the sweat, alcohol, tobacco smoke, and stale air from him. He was still drunk, nearly totally exhausted, and also hungry, yet he felt content and peaceful, and his mind was surprisingly clear.

    Sky was silent and still for several moments, and then he turned around as though distracted. He glanced back and saw some lights flickering on as dawn approached, and he knew that the hard thing to do would be to go back. Back to the village, back to the cramped hotel room and the one-sided conversation of Yasujiro and the beautiful young woman in the dark blue kimono. Back to Yokohama, back to trying to live with the past while hoping for some kind of future with meaning, back to work, friends, love, hatred, relationships that existed beyond his control or understanding, back to Miyako, to everything that she meant to him, and back to the unborn baby girl, who needed and deserved to have two parents. All of these and many more big and little facts of experience made up the overall mystifying mosaic of the hard thing. He had never thought of himself as a brave man, although his government had bestowed upon him citations and decorations to the contrary, but he found the courage to turn around and walk back to the awakening town.

Sky walked back to the village and passed local fishermen going the other way, going down to the sea, as they did every day of their lives. He paused and watched as some of them sailed out into the channel, rolling and tossing among whitecaps in the stiff wind as they approached deep water and eventually became tiny yet still vivid figures on the horizon that was now colored in gradations of red by the slowly rising sun. He walked back to the hotel, where everything was the same as it had been when he left. He threw his few belongings into his cheap, ancient suitcase and headed for the train station, determined to catch the first train for Yokohama.

Chapter Thirty-Five

Ota stopped by the Akabashi one busy Friday night, and it was the first time that Sky had seen him out of his house since his release from the hospital. Sky was glad to see him finally able to get up and around, and he knew how much it must have meant to Ota.

Sky watched Ota dance with Miyumi to a few slow tunes, getting his energy back, easing back into his old routine. He talked with them between sets and asked them to meet him after the last set at a nearby bar. When he met them there after closing time, he was gratified to see Ota in high spirits. He wore a dark suit, a white shirt, and a blue silk tie. He looked tired but contented. As for Miyumi, she looked peaceful yet concerned, and Sky noticed that she was deliberately pacing herself with regard to her drinking. She was a part of the group, but somehow aloof, as if she had a job to do. They sat in the noisy bar, talking and drinking, becoming unaware of the passage of time. They later left the bar and went out on an abbreviated circuit of some of their old haunts. Ota gave the impression of being tireless, as he had always been. Sky figured that he had been saving himself for just such an occasion during his period of recuperation, but he could see that Ota didn't have his former high reserves of energy, and, despite his good spirits, he was wearing down as their night out came to a close.

A Town Where Lights Are Blue

When they finally arrived at Miyumi's house that morning, it was nearly nine o'clock, and they were all drunk, but not in any melancholy way. It was as though they had no troubles, no cares, and no worries about the past or future. It seemed to Sky like a peculiar state of being, given the circumstances of their celebration.

They continued drinking, sitting around the large kotatsu in Miyumi's living room. As the morning began to turn into afternoon, a long silence grew up among them, until at length Ota turned to Sky and spoke. "How're you feeling, John?" he said, and Sky had to give the question some thought, although it seemed simple enough on the surface.

"I mostly feel glad about today being Sunday, old friend," he replied, causing Ota and even the normally reserved Miyumi to laugh. They then restarted their conversation, staying up well into the afternoon. Sky dropped out of the talk around two o'clock, but even after that he could still hear Ota and Miyumi talking in low tones as he drifted from consciousness.

町 光 青

Sky was very tired when he woke up early that evening. He had fallen asleep alongside the *kotatsu*, and he felt sore as he raised himself up. He rubbed his arms and legs for a few moments, trying to speed up the circulation. He wiped his smudged glasses on his tie and combed his hair. He went into the kitchen and saw Miyumi standing by the window watching a light evening rainfall. She was wearing a red silk robe and looked weary but peaceful. She was sipping a cup of tea, her thoughts absorbed by the rain, until she heard

Sky lumbering into the room. She set her teacup down and poured him a cup, which he accepted gratefully. It was hot and strong, and it made him feel more awake almost instantly.

"How do you feel?" she asked softly, finally turning away from watching the rain.

"Terrible. How about you?"

"The same. I'm not used to nights like this anymore," she said, smiling and rubbing her temples.

"Where's Ota? Still sleeping?" he asked, looking at Miyumi. Her eyes were very dark but shining, and there was still a glow of youth in her face, even beneath the hangover and fatigue. She had a kind of beauty that had to be sought out, like a rare and remote treasure, but it was well worth the effort once the goal was achieved.

"Yes, he is. And I intend to see that he stays that way for quite a while. It'll probably take him some time to get used to his old pace again, if that's even possible," she said, and Sky saw a troubled look come across her eyes, clouding them in an intriguing way.

"Something wrong?" he asked, and Miyumi paused, looking as if several thoughts were crossing her mind. She then stepped forward and clasped his arm, but she couldn't bring herself to look at him.

"It's just that he drinks so much, and so do you. Me, too, I guess. Sometimes the two of you drink so much that it seems wrong, very wrong," she said. She then turned around and looked out the window again, her eyes back on the rain, although Sky still had a vivid recollection of the sadness that had come into them while she was speaking. For Miyumi, the few words she had just spoken amounted to giving a speech.

Sky paused, searching for something of meaning to say, ultimately coming up empty on this deceptively simple search. "It doesn't mean anything, Miyumi."

"Oh, it means something, all right, even if I don't have any idea of what it might be. We've been friends for a long time, John. I know that sometimes you drink because you hurt, and it's not just the pain in your leg, or your scars from the war. It's something else, something you never talk about, even to Ota. You drink so much that at times he worries about you, like a brother, even if he'd never tell you or anyone else about it. He doesn't talk about it, but I see it easily enough, in his eyes, in the way he talks about it. As for me, I worry about you, too, just like I worry about him."

"It's not as bad as all that. And, besides, the person we're supposed to be looking out for here is Ota. I can take care of myself. As for him, I know he's got kind of a wild streak in him, but I also know he's got enough common sense to realize that he's got to start taking it easy."

Miyumi nodded as a look of resolve crossed her features. "Oh, make no mistake about it. He will start taking it easy," she said quietly, firmly, and Sky nodded and smiled, feeling good in the knowledge that his best friend was being looked out for by a very good woman.

"Has he said anything to you about going back to work?"

"No. He hasn't mentioned it yet, but I know he thinks about it all the time."

"I know that's got to be true. Well, I'm not going to hang around here any longer. I'd just get in the way. You take it easy yourself, Miyumi. Tell Ota I'll see him again soon, and say that I hope his first night out wasn't too rough on him."

"I'll tell him," Miyumi said, looking around again to face the window. The rain had stopped, and the night was clear and bright with the light of a full moon. She followed him out into the living room and held the door as he got ready to leave.

"You look like you could stand some more sleep," he said.

"You might be right about that. Take care, Sky."

"You, too," he said as he was getting into his coat. Miyumi waved once and turned away, closing the door softly behind her.

A Town Where Lights Are Blue

Chapter Thirty-Six

April started out cold but then evolved into a month of mostly warm weather, despite lingering stretches of cold rain and occasionally biting wind. It was during the first weeks of April that Sky began to notice that Miyako was going through a cycle of change that was subtle yet pronounced. She was still at her job, but she told him that there had been a change in her status. Sky didn't know what this meant, but he didn't press her for details. He took this and the fact that she was spending more time with him and less time at work as signals of better things to come.

Near the middle of April, Sky took Miyako on a trip to some of the smaller towns along the Inland Sea shore of Southern Honshu. He had always wanted to visit this area, but had never found the time. He came to understand that he had always had the time but had managed to find excuses not to go. It was Miyako who gave him the motivation to go, and it became a kind of turning point for both of them, although he couldn't isolate the exact reason why this was so. He just knew that things had changed for them and he accepted this fact. Miyako was especially pleased with the trip. She enjoyed the southbound trip by train, pointing out spots of interest along the way. She was quiet yet animated, content to be doing something energizing and worthwhile. It was during this trip that Sky first noticed that she was no longer consumed by the cold despair that had previously characterized her outlook, although he knew that it hadn't disappeared completely. She now rarely spoke of the sadness evoked by the prospect of growing older, and the deeply ingrained bitterness that was as much a part of her being as her breathing and speech faded as the train moved through the early spring countryside.

It had been necessary for Sky to take a few days off from work in order to make the trip to the Inland Sea, but Tsushima was glad to give him the time off. The few days they spent near the sea would always be fresh and vivid to him. They talked about little things, everyday things, and he finally got around to talking to her about music. He knew that she couldn't really have been very interested in things like chord changes, rim shots, and walking bass techniques, but she was always attentive, and even happy to be sharing in something that was important to him. In turn, Miyako told Sky some of the history of the area, such as the legendary battle of Dannoura that had long ago determined the course that Japanese history would take for hundreds of years to come. She became transformed as she told him stories of the recent and distant past, and the image of her intent look and shining eyes during these monologues instilled in him a feeling of a connection to something old and mysterious, some fundamental yet nearly impossible to understand thing, something well beneath the surface of the modern Japan that he saw every day and had thought he had come to understand.

Sky and Miyako had finished eating dinner in a small, old-fashioned restaurant on a narrow road that stretched between a small fishing village and the sea, and he turned his head and caught a glimpse of her face in profile, her thick black hair blowing in the light evening breeze. Her features were familiar to him but also esoteric, striking in the waning daylight, set in a relaxed yet serious expression that he would always remember. The feeling that he got from this momentary, unplanned image of her, as she walked alongside him dressed in a new *kimono* of pale orange, talking softly, was a sensation of time falling away all around him, a feeling that had nothing to do with bars or high-speed trains or expense accounts or printed circuits or miniskirts or pop music or *pachinko* parlors. It was a feeling that had nothing to do with any kind of day-to-day reality in this country where he knew he was a stranger. What he saw blossoming quietly and spontaneously on Miyako's face as they walked toward the sound of the sea was a look of timeless calm and acceptance, and he was struck by the sensation that, even as she walked close beside him down that dusty road, she was slipping away from him and into something he'd never be able to fully comprehend, and it was at that moment that he genuinely started to know her, the Miyako he had come to know and would know forever, and the Miyako he would never be able to know, and she looked at him and smiled in a way that carried with it traces of a kind of knowledge made up of things like sadness and strength, and it was very clear to him that, whatever roads and reasons had brought them to such a juncture of time and space, he was undeniably in the presence of astonishing beauty.

A Town Where Lights Are Blue

Chapter Thirty-Seven

Sky went deeper into his music, looking for release, trying to forget things he'd always have to remember. The music gave him purpose, and his relationship with the other musicians in the group seemed to solidify as it never had before. He began to truly take charge of the group around this time, although he wasn't aware of this fact. He tried out fresh variations on old songs and came up with suggestions for new material that always worked well in the context of the quartet.

Sky still took trips with his bandmates up and down the coast, but they became less frequent, and when he did go Miyako often accompanied him, although she didn't seem to get much enjoyment out of such journeys. However, he was always grateful for her company when she was able to go along. She was growing more beautiful in his eyes as each day passed, and he began to appreciate the small, simple things they did together, like just talking, going out for meals, or listening to music. He came to realize that she preferred ballads and pop music to jazz or blues, but she was always eager to learn about new things. She would talk with him or sit patiently as he talked music and alcohol and bars with Mikio and Kenji, through a number of chaotic nights, and she occasionally walked with him along bleak, inhospitable stretches of beach as dawn approached.

On a day in late April, Sky was shaken out of an uneasy sleep by a call from Sumiko. Her voice came over the wire in a flat and unemotional tone, telling him that Sayoko was ill and had been admitted to a hospital in Yokohama for a neurological disorder. She gave him the address of the hospital and Sayoko's room number and then hung up without another word. Sky called the hospital and was able to speak to a doctor who had been seeing Sayoko as a patient for a number of years. The doctor told Sky that she had periodic episodes during which she lost motor control and slipped into what looked like an epileptic state, although extensive tests over the years had not shown any signs of this condition. The episodes could come on at any time. There were sometimes only a couple in a year, while during other years there might be several. Medication had been partially effective in minimizing the effects of these events, but in recent years the attacks had been coming more frequently and with greater severity. The most recent one had taken place as she and Sumiko were leaving the cabaret after work. Sayoko had fallen hard onto the pavement and she had suffered serious lacerations and cuts. For a time there had been a fear of concussion, but this had been avoided. The doctor told Sky that in the past Sayoko had been able to recover from her episodes quickly and uneventfully but not this time around. Even after a few days, she was still weak and listless. The doctor told Sky that he couldn't be sure, but there were signs that although he had at one time hoped her condition would improve as she became an adult, it appeared to becoming more debilitating as time passed, beginning with the year she turned twenty-one.

The doctor sounded earnest, exhausted, and saddened by the news he was passing on. Sky thanked him for his willingness to share his insights with him. He then spent a long time sitting in the silence of his house, with no liquor, no tobacco, and no music for company. Sayoko had never spent much time at his home, yet her presence in those moments pervaded every inch of the space around him. Although he would as soon have signed up for another tour of combat duty, he began to make plans to visit the hospital as soon as he could.

A Town Where Lights Are Blue

Chapter Thirty-Eight

Sky walked down the busy hospital corridor, overcome by a feeling of subtle dread. Doctors, nurses, patients, and visitors came and went all around him, talking in low tones or sometimes running toward rooms where emergencies were taking place. He entered Sayoko's room and at first thought he was in the wrong place. The young woman lying in the bed didn't look like Sayoko, at least not at first. He walked over to the bed to take a closer look, and he was shocked when he saw the changes that had come over her. He took a chair from against the wall and pulled it over to the bed. Sayoko at first appeared to be sleeping, but then he saw her eyes flutter open, and she smiled, although not in a way that gave him cause for hope or rejoicing. It was a profoundly sorrowful and resigned smile, the smile of someone who has given up, but only after a long, hard-fought, and bitter struggle.

Sayoko was awake, but she lay still, her skin looking like dark gold against the stark white of the immaculate hospital linen. Her hair was loose, and it fanned out across the crisp pillowcase like a wild, very black storm in heartbreaking disarray. There were dark bruises under both her eyes and a large and ugly cut along her jaw. She looked thin and much older, yet there was still much in evidence about her features a quality of serene and ethereal beauty, and ice flooded into his heart at just the moment he was finally able to look away from her.

"How are you, John Sky?" she said, and the distant, reedy quality of her voice was unnerving.

"I'm doing all right. What about you? How are you doing, Sayoko?" he asked, thinking that words had never come across as more useless or pathetic.

Sayoko gave this question a great deal of thought, and it was some long moments before she responded. "That's not easy to say. I feel peaceful, tired, and old. Can you understand that?"

"I guess not," he replied, and she laughed in a disturbingly lighthearted way.

"I didn't think so."

Sayoko fell silent, as voices drifted past in the corridor, until she began to speak in a slow and deliberate voice, the strength and clarity of which took Sky by surprise. " I knew for a long time that something was wrong with me, but I kept hoping I was mistaken, that I was like everyone else. And of course I'm not. I know that. It was just that I wanted to keep it to myself. I never knew who to talk to about it, until I met you," she said, her tone measured, lucid, empty of affectation or mannerisms. Sky was about to speak when she started talking again. "I'm glad that you stopped by to see me. I wanted the chance to talk to you before I go away. I'm leaving soon, going to America. To New York City."

"That's fine, Sayoko. I mean, if that's what you want. I think that I have to leave soon. I wish you could have told me more about this earlier. I don't know what I could have done to help, but I'd have tried, or asked somebody who could find out how to help. If your leaving makes you happy, then that's good, but I hope your husband is going to take care of you. I'm sorry to talk so much, Sayoko. It's just that I don't understand any of this. I try to never give advice, but this is all wrong for you," Sky said, exhausted now, shaking his head, wanting a cigarette and a glass of whisky. He fell silent, his head down, failing to come up with any more words, even superfluous or pointless ones.

"It was only love, or at least what I took to be love. I'm not sure anymore, but now it's too late. It seemed like the right thing to do at the time, even if it seems crazy now," she said, her voice steady, and then she became quiet again.

Sky turned his head toward her and saw tears trailing down across her cheek, although he couldn't detect any signs of sadness on her face. Sayoko then grabbed his wrist in a grip of surprising strength and spoke to him in a soft, eerie voice. "Please come closer," she said, and he leaned forward until his face was close to hers.

"I know that being a friend of mine isn't an easy thing, but I want you to promise me that, no matter what might ever happen, you'll always be my friend," she said, and sadness came into her face like a silent flood beneath the skin.

"Always, Sayoko, always," he said, quietly but forcefully, and she smiled and turned her face from him as he got up to leave. He walked over to the window and looked out. He saw streets, rooftops, the sea shining in the distance, and this view of Sayoko's town was painful to behold. He stepped back and put his forehead against the cool, smooth surface of the stark white wall, moving it across its coolness as though trying to break a fever. He then stepped away and looked out the window again, the sunshine filling him with anger. His fist exploded through the heavy glass of the window, sounding like low thunder, and he looked at his hand like he'd never seen it before. Sky was a musician, a piano player, yet his hands were rough, almost gnarled in places, the fingers ridged with callus from years of work on his uncle's farm, a million miles away in Montana, rough from falling onto pavement when drunk and clumsy, and scarred by ringworm and unnamed tropical diseases that were as much a part of the Mekong Delta as the water or the heat. He scraped shards of glass away, but he didn't feel any pain. His head cleared, and he saw a nurse coming into the room wearing a stunned expression. He smiled at the serious-looking young nurse, who stepped back and adjusted her glasses, her eyes wide, his smile having unnerved her much more than his brief and pointless act of violence. He walked over to her. "I'm sorry. I didn't mean to do that. I don't have any excuse," he said in a monotone. He then pressed some money into her hand, for fixing the window, for forgiveness, for some reason that was by no means clear to him. She looked at him fearfully as he walked away. Her hand was still holding the crisp bank notes, and she looked at them as though looking through a microscope at some newly discovered organism from a prehistoric age.

Sky walked over to stand beside Sayoko's bed. "Goodbye, Sayo-Chan," he said tenderly, touching her wrist just below a place where white surgical tape secured a tube that had been plunged into her arm. She didn't hear him, but he took comfort in the fact that she appeared to be sleeping peacefully. He walked toward the door, which he saw was filled with the large frame of Sayoko's husband. He nodded toward the man like an old friend and kept walking. The man was about to speak, but Sky spoke first. "Excuse me, but you're in my way," he said civilly, hitting the man high in the chest with his cane, using a thrust like those he had learned from screaming drill sergeants at Fort Leonard Wood when he was a young recruit. The man yelled and then mumbled a few unintelligible words while falling backwards out of the room. Sky stepped over him as he made his way down the corridor, maneuvering through passersby and staff members, wheelchairs, and stretchers, heading for the elevator while the man yelled curses in his direction, although nobody seemed to be listening.

Sky carried with him a deep and pervasive sense of loss that was far greater in intensity than the dull pain in his bleeding right hand. He walked out of the hospital and into a warm spring day now awash in sunshine that felt unpleasantly cold and metallic on his skin. It took him some time to fully comprehend that the thin, broken-looking young woman he had been speaking with in the quiet hospital room really was Sayoko. Sitting with her and being engaged in the almost ritualistic exchange of speech and listening had been like being in on the final, agonizing moments in the life cycle of an exotic creature being destroyed by some capricious force of nature.

The warmth of the April sun and the gentle breeze did nothing to dispel the cold feeling and bitter thoughts that Sky carried with him from the hospital, and the only thing he was able to think about as he walked away was that, her words to the contrary, Sayoko wasn't going to New York City. Sayoko wasn't going anywhere at all. And yet she had already begun to disappear from Yokohama like late afternoon shadows that are absorbed by the coming of night.

A Town Where Lights Are Blue

Chapter Thirty-Nine

Spring had officially arrived, and the weather continued to grow warmer each day, but Sky got the feeling that a long winter was still going on, even if it was slowly coming to an end. He couldn't explain why, but he felt a sense of regret at the passing of this winter. He continued to drink heavily, but he now had a greater awareness of this part of his life. In the past his drinking had been simply another fact of existence, like breathing or not being able to sleep well. Through it all, Miyako remained constant in her understanding of his problem. She knew that there were things he couldn't talk about, not even to her, and that was part of the reason why he drank so much. Her only regret brought on by his drinking was how different he became when he was drunk, almost like a stranger to her, at times a contradiction of his sober self. She knew about this aspect of alcohol, a fact that was often denied or misunderstood.

Whenever Sky was overcome with an urge to get away from Yokohama, he would take Miyako on train trips which, for the most part, she enjoyed. He seldom traveled with his bandmates any more.

Sky and Miyako also spent some nights drinking in the bars of Yokohama, but such occasions were becoming infrequent. As they spent more quiet time with each other, they began to feel less self-conscious about discussing some of the details of their pasts, though neither of them could open up completely. She told him about growing up in the country near Kyoto, and about how she had first worked in a bar in Yokosuka toward the end of the Korean War when she was still a teenager. She had also spent time working in Kobe and Osaka. She was able, in time, to get him to tell her some things about his parents and his years growing up on the Crow Reservation, his early years on the road playing music, and even a little about his army experiences. They learned how to share things. Sky taught her about music and tried to explain why it was so important to him, while Miyako began to introduce him to aspects of Japanese life that he knew little or nothing about. She knew that his main exposure to Japan was through the *mizu shobai*, the "water business"- that subculture made up of the people who worked in the bars and nightspots of the country. Sky was clearly a member of this group, but even he could see that he didn't know much about Japan aside from this. "You know about Japan from somewhere inside you, in a way that even I don't understand, and I think that's good, but now I want you to let me teach you more," she had told him one evening as they worked together preparing dinner, with Mozart's First Piano Concerto playing in the other room. She was lively and gregarious for a change, and the fatigue that had darkened her eyes when she first entered the house that evening had vanished.

Miyako took Sky to *Noh* plays and to a museum where he saw many examples of traditional woodblock prints and the ink drawings known as *sumi-e*. She took him to traditional restaurants and to well-known Yokohama sights that he had never even heard about. He began to realize how in the dark he was about Japan, aside from his round of bars, *ramen* stands, and train stations, but Miyako, in an unassuming way, was beginning to change all that.

Chapter Forty

Ota came by the Akabashi one evening with Miyumi. They arrived just before the end of the next to last set, and Sky went over to visit them during the break. It wasn't long before the beginning of the last set when a waitress came over to tell Sky that he had a phone call, and that he could take it in Tsushima's office. He had a sudden chill as he walked down the corridor toward the office, thinking that the call might be from Sumiko. He walked into the tiny office and sat on the edge of the cluttered desk. The voice on the other end of the wire was flat, uninflected, and empty of any emotion or accent.

"Is this John Sky?"

"Yes. Who's this?"

"Just somebody who knows your name. Haven't you got a girlfriend, an old whore who used to work the bars down in Yokosuka?" the voice asked, and Sky slumped forward.

"What do you want?"

"Me? I don't want anything at all. But, well, your girlfriend, now that's a different matter. She wants you. She's been asking for you. She wants your help, but it's beyond me what kind of help you could give her. I heard that you're kind of a creature of peculiar habits, and I know of a beach down south of the city where the two of you used to take walks every now and then, when the weather was freezing.

She's down there now, and she's waiting for you, and she wants your help." Sky said nothing, as he thought about what was happening, and the voice came on the line again. "Like I said, she's there now, and she's waiting for you, so you might want to make it on down there, soon as you can. Just a piece of advice."

"All right," Sky said, his voice cold, hollow, drained of feeling.

"She'll be waiting for you," the voice said, then paused again. "This is nothing personal, you know." There was then a brief silence before the line went dead, and Sky stood up. He stood by the desk, unable to move, and then left the office. His partners in the band were already on stage, waiting for him. He walked over and motioned to Mikio, who looked confused. He told him to go on without him. Mikio nodded and spoke to the others, and they kicked off the first song of the set, an up-tempo blues. Sky got his jacket and headed for the door, and Ota came over to speak to him.

"What's wrong?"

"I don't know. Maybe it's nothing, but I've got to be sure. It's Miyako. I think something's happened to her. I have to go now."

"I'm going with you."

"You sure you want to?"

"I'm sure. Just let me go tell Miyumi I'm leaving," Ota said, and he walked over to Miyumi, who looked at Sky and frowned, then looked away as Ota walked back across the floor.

Sky and Ota went out to the street and flagged down a taxi, telling the driver to head for Sky's house in a hurry. The driver did as he was told and got them there quickly. On the way across town, Sky filled Ota in with details of the phone call, and he had as clear an idea of what was happening as was possible by the time they arrived at the house. Sky instructed the driver to wait out front, and then hurried inside, Ota following alongside him. Sky went into his plain, Spartan bedroom, turning on the light and heading for the closet. He searched among some boxes on the shelf there until he found what he was looking for-a forty-five caliber automatic pistol and a few clips of ammunition. He had purchased the weapon from a broke and desperate R&R soldier years before and had never known what to do with it once he had it. Ota's eyes widened when he saw this. The gun looked clean and well taken care of. Sky put a magazine into the pistol and pulled the slide back. He then got his overcoat out of the closet and put the pistol into one pocket and the spare clips into the other. Ota noticed that Sky didn't seem nervous or rushed while he was doing this. On the contrary, he came across as sober and methodical, like any working man going out to do a job.

"A gun? I've always known you had some problems, Sky, but this is crazy. Don't you know that you can't own a gun in Japan? Nobody can. Not legally, anyway. They'll deport you for sure if they find you with that thing. Or worse," Ota said, and Sky nodded, appreciating the cool and rational approach Ota was taking to the strange turn of events that had brought an abrupt end to what had started out as a routine night at the Akabashi.

"I can't fault anything you've said. I know that all you say is true. To tell you the truth, I never wanted this thing around, and always figured to get rid of it, legally, if possible. You don't have to worry about it. I won't have it much longer," he said calmly, and Ota glanced at him nervously.

"What do you mean by that?"

Sky paused for a moment. He was sweating, but from pain, not nervousness. He leaned against the wall, taking some of the pressure off his damaged leg, and began to speak in what sounded like a relaxed, conversational way. "Do you remember years ago, when I first came into the B&W? We talked some that night, and you asked about me. I told you I'd only been any good at two things. One of them was music, of course, but then things got busy and I never got to tell you about the second thing. It's shooting. I was good at it from my first time on the rifle range back in basic training. I'd never done it before, and I haven't done it since I left the army, but I was just kind of naturally good at it, right from the start. Doesn't make sense, I guess, but there it is," he said, then began to walk away quickly as he became aware of the time. Ota was stunned by Sky's short speech, but he followed suit and they left the house in a hurry, heading across the yard and into the back seat of the waiting taxi.

町 光 青

Sky said little on the way out of the city, concentrating on giving directions to the driver. He had no trouble getting oriented, although he hadn't been to the remote stretch of beach in several weeks. When they arrived, Sky paid the fare with a handful of bills, and the driver, who was in a hurry to get away as quickly as possible, turned around on the deserted highway and sped back in the direction of the city.

Sky and Ota walked away from the highway toward the sound of the nearby ocean. It was edging toward dawn, but the night was still dark. They walked along until Ota tapped Sky on the shoulder and pointed down the beach, where they could see a dim figure lying near the water's edge. They walked quickly in that direction, and in time they were able to see that the crumpled, unmoving shape lying on the damp sand was Miyako. As the moon slid out of some ragged clouds, Sky was able to discern her features. Her clothes were ripped and spattered with blood, and she had been carelessly covered with a loose-fitting white raincoat. He saw that she had been badly beaten, and the sight of her blood, vivid in the harsh moonlight, filled him for a moment with a feeling so intense that he thought for a moment he might faint. There were cuts on her hands and a huge welt under her left eye. Two fingers of her right hand were mangled and the gold and silver of her many rings, including the plain silver band he had given her, shone darkly through partially dried blood. Her eyes were open and glazed with pain.

"The baby..." she said through torn lips, and Ota looked puzzled. They had never told anyone about the baby, not even him. It had been their secret.

"Don't worry, Miyako. She's going to be fine, and so are you. It's going to be all right. Everything's going to be all right."

"I don't know," she said, her voice scarcely more than a rasping whisper.

"I know. Somebody's hurt you, but we're getting you out of here. We're getting you some help. We're going to help you. We're going to do it."

He looked at her closely and saw that her eyes had suddenly become clear, untouched by any hint of suffering. She looked at him in a searching way. "Are you going to do it?"

"I'm going to do it," he said, and she tried to smile.

"Maria Ayako Sky," she said softly but clearly, and a

shudder went through him. It was the name they had agreed upon for the baby, the baby Miyako insisted would be a girl. That was her department, and Sky never doubted her for a moment. As she had told him once, she was a woman, and women knew about things like that.

"Maria Ayako Sky," he said, as sorrow and caustic rage caused his voice to shake. She looked up at him as a cold sweat coursed through her. Her weak attempt at a smile faded, and her teeth clenched in pain.

"I don't want to be alone anymore," she said, and then began drifting from consciousness.

"You won't be alone anymore."

Miyako couldn't say anything else at the moment, and Sky knelt there holding her, feeling her spasms of pain as they passed through her and came into him. Her breathing was shallow but steady, and as he listened to its rhythmic cadence a cold rage that had been festering beneath his skin came to the surface in a conversely cool and controlled way. It was then that he heard his name being called across the darkness. He motioned to Ota, who took Miyako, and stood up. He set out across the darkened beach, his cane tapping on the packed sand, his right hand grasping the cool metal of the pistol in his coat pocket. It felt completely wrong there, but he stroked it superstitiously, like a totem, a good luck piece, a charm, something as inane and silly to him as any rabbit's foot or four leaf clover would have been. He knew that it was just a tool like any other. One he used long ago, like a post-hole digger or a pitchfork. Just that and nothing more.

The voice that called Sky's name came from the direction of a rocky hill some distance down the beach from where they had found Miyako. He thought that he recognized it as the unfeeling, dispassionate voice he had heard earlier on the phone, but he wasn't sure.

"John Sky? Is that who you are?" the voice called, and by this time Sky stood at the bottom of the short and rocky hill. He looked up, shifting his cane from his left to his right hand and then back again.

"That's me. You've got me at a disadvantage here. Who're you?" he asked, and he could make out the form of an average-sized man holding what looked like some kind of hunting rifle. Sky didn't know much about weapons like that. The only weapons he was familiar with were those used by the army. The rifle was equipped with a scope and looked as exotic to him as a weapon used in space travel. He could also see the loud American, Sayoko's husband, whoever, whatever, he was, standing beside the man. They were both dressed in suits and dark overcoats, just as he was. Sky said nothing as he began walking up the gradual incline of the hill.

"My name's not important. I'm just somebody doing a job. I know your friend down there. He's a lucky man. I usually shoot much better than I did that night," the man said, as though disappointed in himself. Sky said nothing as he continued walking up the hill. He was sweating heavily and grinding his teeth in pain, but he looked on steadily as he kept moving.

"Like I said on the phone, this is nothing personal," the man said, his voice empty.

"I understand. I'm not from the city, like you, but I've been around some all the same. I know how it is. It's only a job, right?"

"That's right. You're smarter than you look, I guess, but not much."

"So, it's just you and me, is that the way of it?"

"It's that way," the man said, shifting his rifle. He then spoke again. "Nothing personal."

Sky reached quickly but carefully for the pistol, clearing the pocket and raising it up and across the darkness, feeling completely in control, as he seldom did, and then only when he was playing music or talking to Miyako. The darkness between him and the top of the hill was momentarily ablaze in flashing light and thundering noise, and then it was quiet again, with only the nearby sound of the surf breaking the silence in an almost metronomic way. Sky saw the rifle, shattered and useless as it fell clattering onto the rocks, fly from the assassin's hands. The man jerked violently, and Sky could see the sick pallor of his skin.

Sky looked at the pistol in his hand, which had been steady but was now shaking imperceptibly. The gunman was standing completely still, like he was waiting for instructions, and his employer was shifting back and forth, for once at a loss for words. Sky felt almost relaxed, though completely exhausted, and he looked back down the hill toward where he had left Miyako and Ota. He then turned around and looked up the hill. He raised the gun and fired quickly, hitting the gunman in both elbows and knees, knocking him backward in a convulsive thrust, screaming in a high, strangled voice as he began to slide down the hill until coming to a stop. He lay with his head pointed down the hill, twitching and gasping in pain. Sky then began walking up the hill. He stopped when he came close to the man. He looked down at him, his eye caught for a moment by the brightness of the streams of blood and splintered bone that punctuated the man's shattered limbs, noticing how the harsh, vivid colors were softened by the waning light of the moon.

"You were wrong," Sky said quietly, lowering the pistol.
"What are you talking about?" the man asked.
"It was personal."
Sky fired twice, putting a round through each of the man's hands. "You won't hurt anybody else. Not with a gun, anyway."

Sky then stood up and followed the gunman's employer up the hill until the man tripped on some loose rocks and fell forward, cutting his forehead. He got up noisily, but he then lay back down, and Sky walked over to him. He fired twice, putting shots close to the man's head and grazing both his ears. The man screamed and grabbed his bleeding ears, then stood up quickly and awkwardly.

"I never knew your name. I don't know who you are, but you'd better get back to wherever you came from and don't come back. And take this man with you," he said, pointing to the ruined assassin. "You get him fixed up. You want people to do your dirty work for you, you best be ready to take care of them if things go wrong," Sky said levelly, and the man went over to the wounded sharpshooter. The gunman screamed once as he was helped to his feet, and his eyes rolled over to white, but then he became silent as he was carried over the crest of the hill.

The sun had almost completely risen as Sky started back across the beach, but there was still a soft hint of moonlight in the sky. He walked down to the tide line and paused, looking at the pistol. He then threw it as far as he could out across the ocean. It broke the water some distance from the shore with hardly a sound to mark its passing. He did the same with the remaining clips of ammunition and then began walking up the beach. He could see that Miyako was somehow standing, although he could see even from a distance that it took a tremendous effort for her to do so. He even thought that she made an effort to wave, but he wasn't certain of this. Looking off to his left, he saw a number of birds flying out across the open sea. The sun was up now, the moonlight had completely faded, and what had felt like a very long night had at last evolved into morning.